THE DONKEY OF GOD

"ON TO PERUGIA!"

See page 96

THE DONKEY OF GOD

BY
LOUIS UNTERMEYER

ILLUSTRATED BY
JAMES MACDONALD

toExcel
San Jose New York Lincoln Shanghai

First published 1935

For my sons

JOHN, JOSEPH AND LANREN

because they are

The Donkey of God

All Rights Reserved. Copyright© 1999 The Estate of Louis Untermeyer.

This edition republished by arrangment with the Estate of Louis Untermeyer, Norma Anchin Untermeyer care of Professional Publishing Services Company and toExcel, a strategic unit of Kaleidscope Software Inc. This permission is expressly granted by Laurence S. Untermeyer.

No part of this book may be reproduced or transmitted in any form or by any means, graphic, electronic or mechanical, including photocopying, recording, taping, or by any information storage or retrieval system, without the permission in writing from the publisher.

For information address:
toExcel
165 West 95th Street, Suite B-N
New York, NY 10025
www.toExcel.com

Published by toExcel, a division of Kaleidoscope Software, Inc.
Marca registrada
toExcel
New York, NY

ISBN: 1-58348-225-3

Library of Congress Catalog Card Number: 99-61565

Printed in the United States of America

0 9 8 7 6 5 4 3 2 1

CONTENTS

Prologue in Naples	3
THE CASTLE THAT CAME OUT OF AN EGG	15
Sorrento—Amalfi—Pompeii	23
THE DOG OF POMPEII	35
Ravello—Salerno—Paestum	53
THE TEMPLE-BOY	65
The Hill-Towns : Orvieto—Perugia—Assisi	81
THE DONKEY OF GOD	95
The Hill-Towns : Gubbio—San Gimignano—Siena	119
THE HORSE OF SIENA	135
Florence	171
THE PAINTED DEATH	197
Venice	229
DAUGHTER OF THE LION	245
Rome	265
THE HOLY CROSS	287

FULL-PAGE ILLUSTRATIONS

" On to Perugia ! "	*frontispiece*
Naples	2
Tell me how to enter an egg without breaking the shell	14
Amalfi	22
It was the end of the world—or so it seemed	34
Paestum	52
—and carried him to the noblest chamber in heaven	64
Assisi	80
So the Archangel Michael called all the animals	94
San Gimignano	118
There were wings, unearthly wings, in the plaza to-day	134
Florence	170
" The picture ! " he gasped. " The painted death ! "	196
Venice	228
Ditta slipped from his clutch and was on the rail	244
Rome	264
A vivid blue light fell upon his face	286

AUTHOR'S APOLOGY

LET me say at once that the legends in this book are not for scholars nor for learned folk who delight in dates and " authorities." They will not find these tales in hand-books or foot-notes for the good reason that this is their first appearance in public. It is, if the truth must be told, almost their first appearance in private ; two years ago the outlines did not exist even in the privacy of a story-teller's mind. Yet, new though they are, the spirit behind them is old—as old as Italy.

The stories had been waiting for me in Italy, that country where there really are sermons in stones—especially since most of the stones have been built up into churches—where poems cluster as thick as olives, where the language is so musical that it is easier to sing the names of villages than to say them, and where every town, tower and mountain-top suggests another tale. The facts of Italy have been told a thousand times ; its stories will never be told. Nor can they be. As fast as they are gathered, others grow ; for every old one, a dozen new ones appear. Legends in Italy are like rabbits—and I doubt if either will ever die out.

It would be pleasant to give some reference or " source " for

AUTHOR'S APOLOGY

these stories. But I am afraid the scholars would find me out. As I hinted before, these tales should not be blamed on any one except myself. Yet they never would have come to me had I not gone to them. I found them—or rather the beginnings of them—in all sorts of places. One was suggested by the plaster-cast of a dog who died almost two thousand years ago; another by the ring in a faded picture in Florence. One almost wrote itself while I stood in the deserted ruins of an ancient temple; another ran by me as I watched a horse-race which was something like a battle and something like a burlesque. One popped out of a castle that had grown ashamed of itself; and one (believe it or not) spoke to me out of the eyes of a dwarf donkey. And there are dozens I never finished, dozens that didn't like my looks or my accent and are waiting for other listeners. There must be hundreds of unborn or half-made stories in Naples alone. And as for the others . . . But let us begin with Naples.

PROLOGUE IN NAPLES

NAPLES

PROLOGUE IN NAPLES

NAPLES was the first Italian town to call me by my first name. I suppose it happens to every one who goes there. Being a busy shipping-port, where the world's great boats are continually coming and going, Naples has no time to waste in getting acquainted. It is touch and go, do or die, all or nothing in Naples. Everything is action, colour, music, surprise. The first glimpse tells all; even the landing at the dock is dramatic.

No harbour in the world is so vivid. The intense sapphire of the sky is matched by the famous Mediterranean blue—as blue as if the mermaids were always washing themselves in blueing. The rose-pink cliffs of the peninsula look like heaped strawberries topped by cream clouds. No wonder that all striped ice-cream is known as Neapolitan!

The human colours are even wilder. The pier is a comic mixture of fantastic costumes: porters in bright jackets; nursemaids with huge lace-caps and gay shawls large as table-cloths; soldiers who might have come out of the toy set that lasted

THE DONKEY OF GOD

from Christmas to New Year's Day; policemen, always in pairs, with three-cornered hats and mysterious capes who seem to be conspirators or a couple of tenors on vacation from the opera. The whole thing looks like a parade that had broken up and could never be put together again.

Most people think of Naples simply as a port of call for those on their way to or from America. But there is something here for every taste. For those who demand scenery that is different, there is the matchless Bay of Naples with its magic islands—Nisida floating near, Ischia disguising itself as a cloud with full sails, Capri rising like a misty sea-monster, changing its shape with every hour. And, above everything, the ever-present Vesuvius, a dream-mountain, in spite of its four thousand stony feet. The panorama from the hilly residential district (the Vomero) is not only too good, but too unreal to be true. You can stop anywhere along the waterfront, turn your head—and see a view to make you gasp. The visitor's chief work in Naples is catching his breath.

For those who like to associate the present with the past, there is a long history that begins with the Greeks who came over in 1050 B.C. and runs through the various Roman Emperors to the victorious entry of Garibaldi. Nero and Hadrian had summer-villas here; here Virgil composed much of his poetry; and here (or, to be exact, around the corner at Pozzuoli) the Apostle Paul landed to spread the Gospel.

PROLOGUE IN NAPLES

For those who are educating themselves in art, there are the antique sculptures, the imposing Castel Nuovo (begun in 1233) with its triumphal arch finished just fifty years before the discovery of America, and the seemingly endless National Museum. This museum is one of the richest in Europe; its picture gallery includes some of the world's greatest paintings; its marble statues have been reproduced in countless plaster images; its bronze figures—most of them taken from the ruins of Pompeii and Herculaneum—are as alive to-day as the latest moving-picture. " The Dancing Faun " is so nimble on his balanced toes that you can almost hear his fingers snap the rhythm; " The Satyr " leans back to empty his heavy wine-skin; the " Mercury Resting " might be any messenger-boy stretching his legs—half relaxed, half resentful—between the newest message and the next. There are, besides, the collections of vases, ancient lamps, jewellery, household utensils and mosaics (those amazing paintings made out of tiny stones) completed twenty centuries ago.

But for most visitors, the chief " sights " of Naples are the Aquarium and the Solfatara. The world is so full of a number of fish in and out of tanks that an aquarium more or less can scarcely matter. Yet the Aquarium at Naples is like no other. Only in Bermuda can you find so strange and curious a collection. Here the impossible has come true; here Nature appears to be playing tricks on itself. Here are fish that seem

THE DONKEY OF GOD

made out of cloudy crystal, so transparent that you can see their delicate silver bones. Here are fish that look like flowers; fish with rainbows on their backs; fish as slender as grass, making themselves invisible in the weeds they hide among; fish with lamps in their tails; fish that find a home in the rock or, to be more exact, go to sleep in dry sand; electric fish that give you a decided shock; calico-fish and flat silk-fish that unroll themselves like a bolt of ribbon; fish like parrots and fish like butterflies; fish with horns; literary fish with black ink in their veins; fish that look like Aunt Minnie and Uncle Jake; bird-fish that fly from coral-branch to branch; fish that seem to be everything except fish. There are more important and imposing places in Naples, but I doubt if any will be remembered longer than the Aquarium.

Utterly different and even more thrilling is a visit to the Solfatara. Popularly known as " Little Vesuvius," it deserves its fearsome name, for the Solfatara is a half-active volcano. You can venture inside the crater with perfect safety—in fact, no visit to Naples is complete without it—and you will have all the excitement of getting acquainted with a live volcano such as Vesuvius without the difficulty and danger. Helped by a guide—and guides in this neighbourhood are thick as flies and almost as annoying—you can find the spots where the ground quivers beneath you and smoke curls out of cracks in the not too-solid earth. You will see pools where mud bubbles

PROLOGUE IN NAPLES

and spouts; you will see the caretaker cook eggs in boiling sand; you will strike your foot on the floor of the crater and will hear hollow echoes come from vast tunnels underneath. The guide will light a torch and columns of sulphur smoke (not as unpleasant as it sounds) will rise from unseen crannies. Here, they say, Dante got his inspiration for the Inferno; and here they will show you the caves which grow hotter as you penetrate their darkness, caves which are supposed to lead to the fiery centre of the universe.

These are the things you are most likely to treasure in memory. But I have two added reasons for remembering Naples. Naples is the place where I saw the castle that had come out of an egg, and it is the place where I first tasted *torrone*. *Torrone* is pronounced to rhyme with macaroni, but it is far different in taste—as different as two tastes can be. *Torrone* is Italy's finest sweetmeat; it is made in a great variety of flavours and is something like an extra-special, super-delicious nougat. It is what nougat would like to be—nougat made by saintly cooks in the candy-shops of Heaven. Only its makers know the remarkable things that go into the slabs that look like thin marble; every maker has a different recipe; and every one swears that his alone is the one genuine, true-to-its-name, wonder-working, strength-giving, death-defying original food of the gods. One way to relish its quality is to cut it into small cubes, eat it slowly, and think of the following legend.

THE DONKEY OF GOD

A great many years ago—or perhaps twice as many—a scientist who also happened to be a great cook was working in the ruins of a Greek temple at Paestum. (A dozen stories could be told about those temples, one of which you will find in this book.) It was as a student of stones, not of cooking, that he was digging, and, after many disappointments, he made an astonishing find.

With the aid of two assistants he removed the dirt of three thousand years and brought to light a magnificent altar in a fine state of preservation. Even more remarkable was the fact that all the objects around it were unbroken; and, after the earth had been cleaned from them, they shone in their own light. There were figured vases and shallow cups and alabaster jars. There were carved pedestals and inlaid knives and a great altar-bowl. And in the centre of the altar-bowl was a slab of something about six inches long and one inch thick. At first the discoverer thought that it was a piece of marble. But when it was exposed to the sun, a curious thing happened: *it bent*. So he took it home and examined it, not in his laboratory, but in his kitchen. There he became the expert cook. He took the mysterious piece to the stove and held it above a charcoal fire. He heated it and treated it, and toasted it and roasted it, and fried it and tried it, and tested it and tasted it.

PROLOGUE IN NAPLES

Finally, when the stuff had cooled, he threw a morsel of it to his mangy old cat who gobbled it up. Then, as he looked, a remarkable change came over his aged pet. Fire came back into the dull green eyes; the drab grey hair grew dark and glossy; the drooping whiskers were transformed into brisk moustaches. In ten minutes the old tom had grown sleek and young and spry. Then the scientist decided it was the original food which the Greek gods ate to keep themselves for ever young—ambrosia they used to call it—and he discovered all the things that went into it and how it had been made. At least he *said* he did. The story tells how he started to manufacture the divine delicacy; and, since he had to buy certain things, a few of the ingredients became known. At the first taste, he recognised a magical sweetness, but it was a sweetness not at all like the common sweetness of sugar. His trained palate told him it was honey, but his skilled taste added it was not an ordinary kind of honey. It took him a long time to discover which flowers and what sort of bees had produced this particular sort. But finally he recognised it as Hybla honey.

Hybla honey is still to be had. But it is hard to get, for it comes from the slopes of Mount Etna, one of the fiercest volcanoes in the world. The ancient gods imprisoned their worst enemy in the pit of the mountain; and whenever the volcano grumbles they say the fire-breathing giant is trying to get out.

THE DONKEY OF GOD

But, although this honey was the base of the gods' food, there were many other ingredients equally hard to find. There were, so this scientist discovered, seven kinds of tropical nuts from seven corners of the world, and the whites of eggs from the whitest pigeons, and the satin hearts of moon-seeds, and cinnamon-powder that had been sifted through silk, and drops of dew from white rose-leaves, and the clear sap of silver gum-trees, and a crumbling of young spices, and the milk of the century-plant that blossoms only once in a hundred years, and five small spirits whose names no one knew.

One day the scientist disappeared. A year went by without a sign of him. At last his family was notified. When his brothers searched the house, they found his recipe for making the ambrosia of eternal youth—all except the names of the five small spirits. They turned the place upside down, inside out, pell-mell, helter-skelter, topsy-turvy, head over heels, cellar to garret. Not a trace; not even the husk of a shell of a single secret seed. In spite of their disappointment, they began to make the candied food—*torrone* they called it. Of course, they couldn't get half of the rare things he used, so they took substitutes—but quite good substitutes. And though it couldn't make people live for ever, it did make them enjoy life more.

No one could deny it—no true *torrone* eater.

That was five hundred years ago. To-day *torrone* is more

PROLOGUE IN NAPLES

popular than ever, even though people have forgotten the man who first made it. And yet, they say, when the full moon shines on the temple at Paestum, a figure comes and stands behind the altar, worshipping the old gods. Some say it is the ghost of the scientist-cook. And others say it is not a ghost at all, but the scientist himself—that he travelled until he got all the ingredients, found out how to make the heavenly ambrosia, and still makes it! So, never growing older, he comes to give thanks, because he shares the secret of the gods, and for him there is no death.

To reach the Castello dell' Ovo you must thread your way through streets that run uphill and through crowds that gather like a storm-cloud about every foreigner. No, crowds don't gather in Naples—half the population of Italy seems to spring up in the middle of a seemingly deserted alley scarcely wide enough for a change of air. You must get used to shouting men, screaming women, and a mixture of chickens, children and household-goats. You will soon realise that the noise is not as bad as it sounds, and that what seems like a murderous argument is only one Neapolitan inviting another to a friendly game of cards.

But it is worth while risking the tumult and the trouble,

THE DONKEY OF GOD

partly for the queer things in the queer streets, partly for the sake of reaching the Castello dell' Ovo. This structure (The Castle of the Egg) is so-called because of its oval shape. History says it was always used as a fort of one kind or another; but legend, which is older and more entertaining than history, gives it a more remarkable origin. A separate chapter has been reserved for " The Castle That Came Out of an Egg." If you will turn the page . . .

TELL ME HOW TO ENTER AN EGG WITHOUT BREAKING THE SHELL

THE CASTLE THAT CAME OUT OF AN EGG

THE CASTLE THAT CAME OUT OF AN EGG

IN the days of B.C. there lived a poet by the name of Virgil. He wrote in Latin, and the people of his day were so well educated that almost every one understood him.

But, besides being a poet, Virgil was a sorcerer, and his enemies said that he had to bewitch people to make them listen to his verses. They even said that his magic wasn't true magic and that his poems were more truth than poetry.

At any rate, the legend has it that Virgil fell completely in love with a lady who thought nothing of his poems and still less of his sorcery. He sent her the most passionate lines and she used the long rolls of parchment to light her fires. He created roses that sang, birds that played musical instruments and answered riddles, tables that decked themselves with food, chairs that slid across the room to wherever she was standing and begged her politely though a little woodenly to be seated.

But she scorned them all. " Tricks ! " she said. " Toys and tricks ! When you can enter an egg without breaking the shell I will believe in you."

THE DONKEY OF GOD

One day Virgil came to a curiously shaped rock on the shore of the Bay of Naples and began counting the waves. When he had counted ninety and nine, he called to a sea-serpent for whom he had done several favours and whose life he had saved when the sea-serpent was a mere worm.

"How can I serve you, Master?" cried the sea-serpent, stretching fifty or sixty of its monstrous coils.

"Tell me how I can enter an egg without breaking the shell," replied Virgil.

"That, Master, is impossible. A man of your size, even though he is a conjurer, could never enter an egg at all. As for anything, even a pin-point, entering it without breaking the shell—why, it's impossible."

"You've said that twice," said Virgil, beginning to lose his temper. "If the thing were possible I wouldn't be coming to you for advice. Didn't I save your life when you were so small that the fishermen were going to put you on their hooks?"

"Yes, Master," replied the sea-serpent meekly.

"And do you want me to change you back to bait again?"

"No, Master," said the sea-serpent with a salt-tear the size of a well in each eye.

"Well, then," said Virgil, "tell me how to do the impossible. Tell me how to enter an egg without breaking the shell."

The sea-serpent looked at the empty sky. Finding nothing

THE CASTLE THAT CAME OUT OF AN EGG

there, it spent fifteen minutes wrinkling and unwrinkling its brow. Then it said, " Give me twenty-seven oysters, tie a cord around the last one, and come back when the moon is full."

It was not the season for oysters, but that did not matter to a conjurer like Virgil. He squeezed lemon juice on twenty-seven round pebbles, threw them to the sea-serpent, and the monster was completely satisfied. Around the twenty-seventh pebble he tied a silk cord and attached one end to the queerly shaped rock. Then he went away.

Three weeks later when the moon was full, Virgil came back to the spot, accompanied by his lady who hid herself as she was told. There was no sign of the sea-serpent. But, carefully balanced on the pointed rock was a new laid sea-serpent's egg of many colours with the silk cord fastened to the inside and the shell unbroken. Quick as a happy thought Virgil changed the frail thread to an iron chain, plucked the rock from its base and anchored it in the sea where it now stands. He then sprinkled the egg with seven kinds of water and repeated an Arabian incantation, though his accent was not the purest. Then he said :

" By magic this egg was born ; by magic let it be transformed. Let this egg stand for ever. Let its colours separate into rooms surpassing in brilliance all the others since the palace of Aladdin. Let each drop within it change into tapestries and precious stuffs, jewelled glasses, diamond windows. Let this

THE DONKEY OF GOD

brittle shell grow into unbreakable walls, resisting all enemies. And let it come to pass before I end the charm."

Even as he said the words, the egg swelled, rose, hardened itself into walls, and towered above the bay. There was not a crack in it anywhere until a door opened and trumpeters spoke from the turrets. Troops poured forth: archers and swordsmen and cavalry, all bearing the emblem of the sea-serpent's egg. "Enter," called a voice that sounded from the depths of the sea. "Enter," cried the troops and the trumpeters. "Enter, O enchanter, and rule behind walls that never can be broken!"

At that moment, the lady started up from her hiding-place. She had seen with astonished eyes each step of the transformation. "I believe!" she cried, throwing her arms about Virgil. "I am yours for ever. I believe you now!"

But Virgil freed his neck of her arms. "It doesn't matter now whether you believe me or not," he said with a shrug. "If I have to convince people with miracles, I'll do it in my own way."

And he went back to his poetry.

Thus the legend. To those who refuse to believe it, I may remark that The Castle That Came Out of an Egg is still standing on the shore at Naples and that its shell is still unbroken. And, for a further proof, there are the poems of Virgil which have outlasted most of the palaces of the world.

THE CASTLE THAT CAME OUT OF AN EGG

I should add that it doesn't look much like an enchanted castle to-day. For a long time it was uninhabited. One can hardly blame people for refusing to live in it. There was always the chance that Virgil, or his ghost, might come along and reverse the spell. And where would you be if the building you were living in suddenly decided to be an egg again—and a sea-serpent's egg at that—fond of the bottom of the bay?

History now takes the place of legend and records show that the egg-shaped castle became a villa where Julius Caesar was entertained, a fort as early as 1150, and finally a military prison. For hundreds of years, it has been used as a jail. But the origin is still celebrated by the jailers. The chief diet of the prisoners, they say, is eggs.

SORRENTO—AMALFI—POMPEII

AMALFI

SORRENTO—AMALFI—POMPEII

SOME one has said that the best thing about going to Naples is going to Pompeii. There is some truth in the saying, but there are many things within the city and outside of its borders that no one should miss. There is the drive along the waterfront, past the famous island of Nisida to the ancient Roman resort of Baia, where the bathers and pleasure-seekers came two thousand years ago and the Temple of Venus is still standing. There is the rock-island of Capri, whose bold colours, toy-houses and brilliant caves attract artists from every corner of the world; the Blue Grotto, which is a watery fairyland of sapphire and silver, works its magic way under the hills, and on these slopes the Emperor Tiberius came to spend the last years of his life. Above all, there is the never-to-be-forgotten Sorrento-Amalfi drive.

In these days of high-powered motor-cars, the Sorrento-Amalfi drive can be accomplished in a single day, stopping at Sorrento for lunch, Amalfi for tea and getting back to Naples for dinner. But it is far better to spend a few days on

THE DONKEY OF GOD

the way and learn to know a part of Italy different from any other.

Sorrento has one of the most picturesque locations in this picturesque world. Rising on sheer cliffs above the sea, Sorrento seems to be standing on its toes with its elbows on the hills and its head among the clouds. The hotels are hundreds of feet above the little landing-place and have their own elevators cut down through solid rock. In spring the town is full of Americans and English; in summer the streets are sultry with the sirocco, the hot, dry wind that carries the sand of Africa clear across the sea. But there are the long, sweeping beaches and the old-fashioned bath-houses with let-down ladders to pull up after you, and the lace factories, and the little shops where they make the *intarsia* work for which Sorrento is famous—tables and book-racks and boxes for every purpose inlaid with thin pieces of many-coloured woods. And, every evening, in the courtyard of one inn or another, there is the tarantella.

The tarantella should not be confused with the tarantula, a poisonous insect, although some one has said that the first is the result of being bitten by the second. The tarantella, which originated in the Mediterranean villages, has come to be the national dance of Italy. It is really not one dance, but a combination of several dances and many moods. Usually performed by a couple, the tarantella is a love-story accompanied by music; it generally has the aid of a chorus, tambourines and those little wooden hand-cymbals called castanets. As the tune rises and falls the lovers court and quarrel; he threatens and she pouts; he advances, she retreats; he offers gifts, she half-accepts, half-spurns them; he storms, accuses, cries, coaxes. Finally, she consents, and the dance winds up in a general jubilation in which the musicians—and often the onlookers—join. Then every one goes to sip something sweet and, if the moon is to be relied upon, stroll home through a story-book world.

Amalfi, like Caesar's Gaul, is divided into three parts: the part that centres about the large hotel which used to be a monastery, the section of romantic outlooks celebrated by poets and painters, and the village itself whose chief business (apart from the tourists) is fish. The fishing at Amalfi is like no other anywhere; it is partly a means of livelihood, partly a social custom, and it is done at night. When it is dark, a fleet of long boats may be noticed leaving the shore for deep water. They can be barely seen and never heard—not, at least, on the way out—for the fish must not be frightened away. The boats, with nets between them, pull slowly toward the fishing-grounds, silently, invisibly. Suddenly lights begin bobbing up and down the water; the sea dances with them. These are torches, and they are used to attract the fish as well as to allow the fishermen to see what they are doing.

THE DONKEY OF GOD

All is noise and action now. The nets are hauled in; jokes fly from boat to boat; the little engines cough their fastest putt-putt-putt; the vessels are beached with cries that sound like threats of murder, but which are only comparisons of the size of the haul. Then, and only then, the village of Amalfi is allowed to go to sleep.

Sometimes, that is. Usually, as soon as the fishermen cease, the bells begin. There are, I believe, as many bells in Amalfi as there are fish in its waters or tourists in its hotels. I imagine, though I can't be positive, that every time another visitor comes to town, another bell is hung and rung. And at the height of the season—! Besides bells that strike the hours, there are bells for vespers, bells for early mass—and early mass in Amalfi seems to take place in the middle of the night—bells for breakfast, bells for prayers, bells for hot water, bells to announce the coming, the arrival and the departure of every guest, bells in balconies, boat-houses and belfries, bells that ring for the sheer fun of ringing. Everything in Amalfi goes to

> The clanging and the twanging
> And the swinging and the ringing
> And the wrangling and the jangling
>   Of the bells, bells, bells,
> Of the bells, bells, bells, bells, bells, bells. . . .

SORRENTO—AMALFI—POMPEII

I should add that there are no small or peaceful chimes in Amalfi. On the contrary; every bell believes in striking while its iron is hot. And every bell tries to outdo every other bell in force, volume, and duration. I sometimes suspect that the men who pull the ropes regard the whole thing as a contest and that every boy born in Amalfi wants to be known as The Longest and Loudest Bell-Ringer in Europe.

But bells and fish are not the only diversions in Amalfi. They should not be mentioned first, but last. The first thing any one does is to go up to the Capuchin Convent which, between its flowered pillars, commands one of the grandest of views. Once a lofty monastery, it has been made over into a luxurious hotel. And here, where the monks did penance on water and dry crusts, you are offered a sumptuous tea with rich cakes. Nor do you have to climb the rocky slope that bruised the Capuchins' feet. There are a few hundred steps, it is true; but you can manage these without much trouble, or, if you are either tired or very rich, you can be carried up in a sort of sedan-chair basket by two priestly porters. The view— But I am not foolish enough to try to paint the impossible in words.

Amalfi itself is backed by a fortress of mountains. The town is perched on the sides so steeply that it seems in constant danger of sliding off into the sea. The houses seem to be built on each other's roofs. The colours, the shapes, the very placing

THE DONKEY OF GOD

of the town seem to have been done by a child with a set of blocks, some coloured tiles, and a sense of humour. Some one, I thought, when I first saw Amalfi from the water—the best way to get the effect, by the bye—some one must have had a good time piling those pink and blue buildings on top of each other. . . .

> Some one weary of all styles
>   Architects must master,
> Some one with a box of tiles
>   And a pinch of plaster,
>
> Some one, part a child, and part
>   A poet touched with malice,
> Some one with a laughing heart
>   Planned these coloured alleys.
>
> Like the prows of gaudy skiffs
>   Roofs were tossed; he ran his
> Houses up impossible cliffs
>   And the craziest crannies.
>
> Piled the town upon itself
>   With a nimble mockery,
> Till it seemed like shelf on shelf
>   Of peasant crockery.

SORRENTO—AMALFI—POMPEII

> Roads to slip uphill he bent
> > Rapidly in slow air;
> Roads that crossed themselves and went
> > Neatly into nowhere.
>
> Here a tower, there a wall,
> > A church, a stoop, a steeple.
> Then, the liveliest touch of all,
> > He put in the people.

The people are Amalfi's quaintest decorations. Wholly unlike the shop-keepers of the larger cities, they are interested in strangers for their own sake, not merely for the sake of their money. I remember an old woman who sold vegetables in the market square; she must have been eighty years old, but she carried her basket of cabbages upon her head as though it were the crown of a duchess. I asked her if she had ever been in America and she replied that one of her sons was "a great man" with his own carriage in Brooklyn. Later I found out he drove an ice-wagon. "Besides," she went on, "why should I go to America when the best of America comes to Italy?" To this day I cannot tell whether her question was a general remark or a personal compliment.

Then, in addition to all these attractions, there are the tiny shops, the village letter-writers, the eleventh-century cathedral of Saint Andrea with its noble flight of steps, the waterfalls at the Valley of the Mills, the ascent to Ravello. . . . But here you are faced with two choices. One leads you further south, to Salerno and the temples at Paestum; the other takes you in a half-circle to Pompeii. Let us keep Paestum for another day and go, as every visitor must, to the most famous ruins of their kind.

There are several ways of going to Pompeii. Many travellers prefer seeing the ruins as a climax to the Sorrento-Amalfi drive, but the easiest method is direct from Naples. It used to be a difficult journey, most of the day in a carriage or two hours in a groaning antique automobile over a road that seemed more ruined than the ruins themselves. But now there is a magnificent motor-speedway, and the cars skim over it in less than twenty minutes. You leave your hotel, settle yourself comfortably, and before you can say Marcus Aurelius —though, of course, it isn't necessary to say it—you are at the entrance to what is left of Pompeii.

The first glance is disappointing. Pompeii is just the shell of a city: the houses are bare of furnishings, the streets without decorations, the temples have been robbed of their statues. But the very bareness is impressive, and the imagination re-

SORRENTO — AMALFI — POMPEII

constructs the scene when, seventy-nine years after the birth of Jesus, the top of Vesuvius blew off and the volcano vomited red-hot stones, fiery ashes and suffocating fumes, burying the tallest roof-tops of the town for eighteen centuries. Imagination, also, must fill these streets with the gaily dressed men and women who made the town a by-word for pleasure, with foreign adventurers and local officials, portly priests and lean Roman soldiers, merchants and marauders, citizens and slaves, children and dogs. You will find some of these, at least, in the tale that I have called " The Dog of Pompeii."

THE DOG OF POMPEII

IT WAS THE END OF THE WORLD—OR SO IT SEEMED

THE DOG OF POMPEII

TITO and his dog Bimbo lived (if you could call it living) under the wall where it joined the inner gate. They really didn't live there; they just slept there. They lived anywhere. Pompeii was one of the gayest of the old Latin towns, but although Tito was never an unhappy boy, he was not exactly a merry one. The streets were always lively with shining chariots and bright red trappings; the open-air theatres rocked with laughing crowds; sham-battles and athletic sports were free for the asking in the great stadium. Once a year the Caesar visited the pleasure-city and the fire-works lasted for days; the sacrifices in the Forum were better than a show. But Tito saw none of these things. He was blind—had been blind from birth. He was known to every one in the poorer quarters. But no one could say how old he was, no one remembered his parents, no one could tell where he came from. Bimbo was another mystery. As long as people could remember seeing Tito—about twelve or thirteen years—they had seen Bimbo. Bimbo had never left his side. He was not only dog, but nurse, pillow, playmate, mother and father to Tito.

Did I say Bimbo never left his master? (Perhaps I had better say comrade, for if any one was the master, it was Bimbo.) I was wrong. Bimbo did trust Tito alone exactly three times a day. It was a fixed routine, a custom understood between boy and dog since the beginning of their friendship, and the way it worked was this: Early in the morning, shortly after dawn, while Tito was still dreaming, Bimbo would disappear. When Tito woke, Bimbo would be sitting quietly at his side, his ears cocked, his stump of a tail tapping the ground, and a fresh-baked bread—more like a large round roll—at his feet. Tito would stretch himself; Bimbo would yawn; then they would breakfast. At noon, no matter where they happened to be, Bimbo would put his paw on Tito's knee and the two of them would return to the inner gate. Tito would curl up in the corner (almost like a dog) and go to sleep, while Bimbo, looking quite important (almost like a boy) would disappear again. In half an hour he'd be back with their lunch. Sometimes it would be a piece of fruit or a scrap of meat, often it was nothing but a dry crust. But sometimes there would be one of those flat rich cakes, sprinkled with raisins and sugar, that Tito liked so much. At supper-time the same thing happened, although there was a little less of everything, for things were hard to snatch in the evening with the streets full of people. Besides, Bimbo didn't approve of

THE DOG OF POMPEII

too much food before going to sleep. A heavy supper made boys too restless and dogs too stodgy—and it was the business of a dog to sleep lightly with one ear open and muscles ready for action.

But, whether there was much or little, hot or cold, fresh or dry, food was always there. Tito never asked where it came from and Bimbo never told him. There was plenty of rain-water in the hollows of soft stones; the old egg-woman at the corner sometimes gave him a cupful of strong goat's milk; in the grape-season the fat wine-maker let him have drippings of the mild juice. So there was no danger of going hungry or thirsty. There was plenty of everything in Pompeii, if you knew where to find it—and if you had a dog like Bimbo.

As I said before, Tito was not the merriest boy in Pompeii. He could not romp with the other youngsters and play Hare-and-Hounds and I-spy and Follow-your-Master and Ball-against-the-Building and Jack-stones and Kings-and-Robbers with them. But that did not make him sorry for himself. If he could not see the sights that delighted the lads of Pompeii he could hear and smell things they never noticed. He could really see more with his ears and nose than they could with their eyes. When he and Bimbo went out walking he knew just where they were going and exactly what was happening.

"Ah," he'd sniff and say, as they passed a handsome villa,

THE DONKEY OF GOD

"Glaucus Pansa is giving a grand dinner to-night. They're going to have three kinds of bread, and roast pigling, and stuffed goose, and a great stew—I think bear-stew—and a fig-pie." And Bimbo would note that this would be a good place to visit to-morrow.

Or, "H'm," Tito would murmur, half through his lips, half through his nostrils. "The wife of Marcus Lucretius is expecting her mother. She's shaking out every piece of goods in the house; she's going to use the best clothes—the ones she's been keeping in pine-needles and camphor—and there's an extra girl in the kitchen. Come, Bimbo, let's get out of the dust!"

Or, as they passed a small but elegant dwelling opposite the public-baths, "Too bad! The tragic poet is ill again. It must be a bad fever this time, for they're trying smoke-fumes instead of medicine. Whew! I'm glad I'm not a tragic poet!"

Or, as they neared the Forum, "Mm-m! What good things they have in the Macellum to-day!" (It really was a sort of butcher-grocer-market-place, but Tito didn't know any better. He called it the Macellum.) "Dates from Africa, and salt oysters from sea-caves, and cuttlefish, and new honey, and sweet onions, and—ugh!—water-buffalo steaks. Come, let's see what's what in the Forum." And Bimbo, just as curious as his comrade, hurried on. Being a dog, he trusted his ears and nose (like Tito) more than his eyes. And so the two of them entered the centre of Pompeii.

THE DOG OF POMPEII

The Forum was the part of the town to which everybody came at least once during each day. It was the Central Square and everything happened here. There were no private houses; all was public—the chief temples, the gold and red bazaars, the silk shops, the town hall, the booths belonging to the weavers and jewel merchants, the wealthy woollen market, the shrine of the household gods. Everything glittered here. The buildings looked as if they were new—which, in a sense, they were. The earthquake of twelve years ago had brought down all the old structures and, since the citizens of Pompeii were ambitious to rival Naples and even Rome, they had seized the opportunity to rebuild the whole town. And they had done it all within a dozen years. There was scarcely a building that was older than Tito.

Tito had heard a great deal about the earthquake though, being about a year old at the time, he could scarcely remember it. This particular quake had been a light one—as earthquakes go. The weaker houses had been shaken down, parts of the out-worn wall had been wrecked; but there was little loss of life, and the brilliant new Pompeii had taken the place of the old. No one knew what caused these earthquakes. Records showed they had happened in the neighbourhood since the beginning of time. Sailors said that it was to teach the lazy city-folk a lesson and make them appreciate those who risked the dangers of the sea to bring them luxuries and pro-

THE DONKEY OF GOD

tect their town from invaders. The priests said that the gods took this way of showing their anger to those who refused to worship properly and who failed to bring enough sacrifices to the altars and (though they didn't say it in so many words) presents to the priests. The tradesmen said that the foreign merchants had corrupted the ground and it was no longer safe to traffic in imported goods that came from strange places and carried a curse with them. Every one had a different explanation—and every one's explanation was louder and sillier than his neighbour's.

They were talking about it this afternoon as Tito and Bimbo came out of the side-street into the public square. The Forum was the favourite promenade for rich and poor. What with the priests arguing with the politicians, servants doing the day's shopping, tradesmen crying their wares, women displaying the latest fashions from Greece and Egypt, children playing hide-and-seek among the marble columns, knots of soldiers, sailors, peasants from the provinces—to say nothing of those who merely came to lounge and look on—the square was crowded to its last inch. His ears even more than his nose guided Tito to the place where the talk was loudest. It was in front of the Shrine of the Household Gods that, naturally enough, the householders were arguing.

" I tell you," rumbled a voice which Tito recognised as bath-master Rufus's, " there won't be another earthquake in my

THE DOG OF POMPEII

lifetime or yours. There may be a tremble or two, but earthquakes, like lightnings, never strike twice in the same place."

"Do they not?" asked a thin voice Tito had never heard. It had a high, sharp ring to it and Tito knew it as the accent of a stranger. "How about the two towns of Sicily that have been ruined three times within fifteen years by the eruptions of Mount Etna? And were they not warned? And does that column of smoke above Vesuvius mean nothing?"

"That?" Tito could hear the grunt with which one question answered another. "That's always there. We use it for our weather-guide. When the smoke stands up straight we know we'll have fair weather; when it flattens out it's sure to be foggy; when it drifts to the east—"

"Yes, yes," cut in the edged voice. "I've heard about your mountain barometer. But the column of smoke seems hundreds of feet higher than usual and it's thickening and spreading like a shadowy tree. They say in Naples—"

"Oh, Naples!" Tito knew this voice by the little squeak that went with it. It was Attilio, the cameo-cutter. "*They* talk while we suffer. Little help we got from them last time. Naples commits the crimes and Pompeii pays the price. It's become a proverb with us. Let them mind their own business."

"Yes," grumbled Rufus, "and others, too."

"Very well, my confident friends," responded the thin voice

THE DONKEY OF GOD

which now sounded curiously flat. " We also have a proverb—and it is this : Those who will not listen to men must be taught by the gods. I say no more. But I leave a last warning. Remember the holy ones. Look to your temples. And when the smoke-tree above Vesuvius grows to the shape of an umbrella-pine, look to your lives."

Tito could hear the air whistle as the speaker drew his toga about him and the quick shuffle of feet told him the stranger had gone.

" Now what," said the cameo-cutter, " did he mean by that ? "

" I wonder," grunted Rufus, " I wonder."

Tito wondered, too. And Bimbo, his head at a thoughtful angle, looked as if he had been doing a heavy piece of pondering. By nightfall the argument had been forgotten. If the smoke had increased no one saw it in the dark. Besides, it was Caesar's birthday and the town was in holiday mood. Tito and Bimbo were among the merry-makers, dodging the charioteers who shouted at them. A dozen times they almost upset baskets of sweets and jars of Vesuvian wine, said to be as fiery as the streams inside the volcano, and a dozen times they were cursed and cuffed. But Tito never missed his footing. He was thankful for his keen ears and quick instinct—most thankful of all for Bimbo.

They visited the uncovered theatre and, though Tito could not see the faces of the actors, he could follow the play better than most of the audience, for their attention wandered—they were distracted by the scenery, the costumes, the by-play, even by themselves—while Tito's whole attention was centred in what he heard. Then to the city-walls, where the people of Pompeii watched a mock naval-battle in which the city was attacked by the sea and saved after thousands of flaming arrows had been exchanged and countless coloured torches had been burned. Though the thrill of flaring ships and lighted skies was lost to Tito, the shouts and cheers excited him as much as any and he cried out with the loudest of them.

The next morning there were *two* of the beloved raisin and sugar cakes for his breakfast. Bimbo was unusually active and thumped his bit of a tail until Tito was afraid he would wear it out. The boy could not imagine whether Bimbo was urging him to some sort of game or was trying to tell something. After a while, he ceased to notice Bimbo. He felt drowsy. Last night's late hours had tired him. Besides, there was a heavy mist in the air—no, a thick fog rather than a mist—a fog that got into his throat and scraped it and made him cough. He walked as far as the marine gate to get a breath of the sea. But the blanket of haze had spread all over the bay and even the salt air seemed smoky.

He went to bed before dusk and slept. But he did not sleep well. He had too many dreams—dreams of ships lurching in the Forum, of losing his way in a screaming crowd, of armies

THE DONKEY OF GOD

marching across his chest, of being pulled over every rough pavement of Pompeii.

He woke early. Or, rather, he was pulled awake. Bimbo was doing the pulling. The dog had dragged Tito to his feet and was urging the boy along. Somewhere. Where, Tito did not know. His feet stumbled uncertainly; he was still half asleep. For a while he noticed nothing except the fact that it was hard to breathe. The air was hot. And heavy. So heavy that he could taste it. The air, it seemed, had turned to powder, a warm powder that stung his nostrils and burned his sightless eyes.

Then he began to hear sounds. Peculiar sounds. Like animals under the earth. Hissings and groanings and muffled cries that a dying creature might make dislodging the stones of his underground cave. There was no doubt of it now. The noises came from underneath. He not only heard them—he could feel them. The earth twitched; the twitching changed to an uneven shrugging of the soil. Then, as Bimbo half-pulled, half-coaxed him across, the ground jerked away from his feet and he was thrown against a stone-fountain.

The water—hot water—splashing in his face revived him. He got to his feet, Bimbo steadying him, helping him on again. The noises grew louder; they came closer. The cries were even more animal-like than before, but now they came from human throats. A few people, quicker of foot and more hurried by

THE DOG OF POMPEII

fear, began to rush by. A family or two—then a section—then, it seemed, an army broken out of bounds. Tito, bewildered though he was, could recognise Rufus as he bellowed past him, like a water-buffalo gone mad. Time was lost in a nightmare.

It was then the crashing began. First a sharp crackling, like a monstrous snapping of twigs; then a roar like the fall of a whole forest of trees; then an explosion that tore earth and sky. The heavens, though Tito could not see them, were shot through with continual flickerings of fire. Lightnings above were answered by thunders beneath. A house fell. Then another. By a miracle the two companions had escaped the dangerous side-streets and were in a more open space. It was the Forum. They rested here awhile—how long he did not know.

Tito had no idea of the time of day. He could *feel* it was black—an unnatural blackness. Something inside—perhaps the lack of breakfast and lunch—told him it was past noon. But it didn't matter. Nothing seemed to matter. He was getting drowsy, too drowsy to walk. But walk he must. He knew it. And Bimbo knew it; the sharp tugs told him so. Nor was it a moment too soon. The sacred ground of the Forum was safe no longer. It was beginning to rock, then to pitch, then to split. As they stumbled out of the square, the earth wriggled like a caught snake and all the columns of the temple of Jupiter came down. It was the end of the world—or so it seemed.

THE DONKEY OF GOD

To walk was not enough now. They must run. Tito was too frightened to know what to do or where to go. He had lost all sense of direction. He started to go back to the inner gate; but Bimbo, straining his back to the last inch, almost pulled his clothes from him. What did the creature want? Had the dog gone mad?

Then, suddenly, he understood. Bimbo was telling him the way out—urging him there. The sea gate of course. The sea gate—and then the sea. Far from falling buildings, heaving ground. He turned, Bimbo guiding him across open pits and dangerous pools of bubbling mud, away from buildings that had caught fire and were dropping their burning beams. Tito could no longer tell whether the noises were made by the shrieking sky or the agonised people. He and Bimbo ran on—the only silent beings in a howling world.

New dangers threatened. All Pompeii seemed to be thronging toward the marine gate and, squeezing among the crowds, there was the chance of being trampled to death. But the chance had to be taken. It was growing harder and harder to breathe. What air there was choked him. It was all dust now—dust and pebbles, pebbles as large as beans. They fell on his head, his hands—pumice-stones from the black heart of Vesuvius. The mountain was turning itself inside out. Tito remembered a phrase that the stranger had said in the Forum two days ago: " Those who will not listen to men must be taught

THE DOG OF POMPEII

by the gods." The people of Pompeii had refused to heed the warnings; they were being taught now—if it was not too late.

Suddenly it seemed too late for Tito. The red hot ashes blistered his skin, the stinging vapours tore his throat. He could not go on. He staggered toward a small tree at the side of the road and fell. In a moment Bimbo was beside him. He coaxed. But there was no answer. He licked Tito's hands, his feet, his face. The boy did not stir. Then Bimbo did the last thing he could—the last thing he wanted to do. He bit his comrade, bit him deep in the arm. With a cry of pain, Tito jumped to his feet, Bimbo after him. Tito was in despair, but Bimbo was determined. He drove the boy on, snapping at his heels, worrying his way through the crowd; barking, baring his teeth, heedless of kicks or falling stones. Sick with hunger, half-dead with fear and sulphur-fumes, Tito pounded on, pursued by Bimbo. How long he never knew. At last he staggered through the marine gate and felt soft sand under him. Then Tito fainted. . . .

Some one was dashing sea-water over him. Some one was carrying him toward a boat.

"Bimbo," he called. And then louder, "Bimbo!" But Bimbo had disappeared.

Voices jarred against each other. "Hurry—hurry!" "To the boats!" "Can't you see the child's frightened and starving!"

THE DONKEY OF GOD

" He keeps calling for some one ! " " Poor boy, he's out of his mind." " Here, child—take this ! "

They tucked him in among them. The oar-locks creaked ; the oars splashed ; the boat rode over toppling waves. Tito was safe. But he wept continually.

" Bimbo ! " he wailed. " Bimbo ! Bimbo ! "

He could not be comforted.

Eighteen hundred years passed. Scientists were restoring the ancient city ; excavators were working their way through the stones and trash that had buried the entire town. Much had already been brought to light—statues, bronze instruments, bright mosaics, household articles ; even delicate paintings had been preserved by the fall of ashes that had taken over two thousand lives. Columns were dug up and the Forum was beginning to emerge.

It was at a place where the ruins lay deepest that the Director paused.

" Come here," he called to his assistant. " I think we've discovered the remains of a building in good shape. Here are four huge mill-stones that were most likely turned by slaves or mules—and here is a whole wall standing with shelves inside it. Why ! It must have been a bakery. And here's a curious thing. What do you think I found under this heap where the ashes were thickest ? The skeleton of a dog ! "

THE DOG OF POMPEII

" Amazing ! " gasped his assistant. " You'd think a dog would have had sense enough to run away at the time. And what is that flat thing he's holding between his teeth ? It can't be a stone."

" No. It must have come from this bakery. You know it looks to me like some sort of cake hardened with the years. And, bless me, if those little black pebbles aren't raisins. A raisin-cake almost two thousand years old ! I wonder what made him want it at such a moment ? "

" I wonder," murmured the assistant.

RAVELLO—SALERNO—PAESTUM

PAESTUM

RAVELLO — SALERNO — PAESTUM

WHEN I first told the story of "The Dog of Pompeii" to an audience of one, I was immediately asked what happened to Tito. I was embarrassed, for I was not at all sure, and it seemed foolish for a story-teller not to know what became of his own people. Since that time I have thought a bit about it; and this, it seems to me, is what must have occurred.

The people who rescued the blind Tito must have brought him to Naples. There, I am sure, he attracted attention and was adopted by a childless couple, who took him to Rome. As Tito grew up, his cleverness showed itself in a dozen ways, but especially in anything connected with animals. Wild or tame, it didn't matter to Tito. He had what is called "the healing hand," and the things he accomplished with beasts were unbelievable.

His reputation grew so great that when the court-physicians failed to heal the favourite cat of Caesar's wife—she was a Royal Persian—(the cat was—not Caesar's wife)—some one sent for Tito. Of course he cured her and the Empress gave

THE DONKEY OF GOD

him a collar of many jewels. Then the sacred bull that belonged to the temple of Jupiter got a kind of fever, foamed at the mouth and lashed his tail like an evil dragon. Tito fed him the hearts of a certain plant and in two weeks the bull's white hide was silkier and his brown eyes softer than ever. So they made Tito a priest and gave him a great house of his own. Soon it was discovered that there were no more mad dogs in Rome. Tito had seen to it that fresh water and tidbits were left out for all the homeless ones. All during his life the Romans sang his praises. Upon his death it was found that Tito had left all his money to care for neglected animals and his countrymen erected a statue to his memory. Under his name some poet had added this line : " He did not need eyes who had an all-seeing heart." The statue showed a young man seated, and at his feet, with one paw laid on his knee, was the image of a dog looking very much like Bimbo.

And what became of Bimbo ? That is somewhat harder to answer, especially since I am not certain what a dog's Heaven is like. But I do know this : You can see more of Bimbo to-day than you can of Tito. Tito's body went to dust and he was remembered only by his statue. Then even the statue went; worn by wind and rain, thrown down during many wars. Tito's statue crumbled hundreds of years ago.

But Bimbo's remains have been kept very carefully. A few years ago, when the Director of Antiquities began working in

RAVELLO—SALERNO—PAESTUM

the ashes of Pompeii, he saw that the eighteen-hundred-year-old bodies decayed the moment they were exposed to the air, leaving only a few bones. But he also noticed that each body left a perfect impression in the ashes which had hardened. The impressions were as good as moulds—in fact, they *were* moulds. So the Director filled these natural moulds with soft plaster of Paris and made casts as fine as any statue. That was how he preserved Bimbo. Any one going to Pompeii will find him lying just as he was discovered, lying in the most important glass case in the Museum.

Resuming the trip further south (as I hope you will), Ravello is decidedly a place to visit. It is reached from Amalfi. In fact it towers above the small sea-port like the hanging gardens of Babylon, or, as Richard Wagner wrote in the guest-book of Ravello's chief hotel, like the enchanted garden of Klingsor in " Parsifal " which vanished from earth but which, said Wagner, came back here. Ravello is something out of a sorcerer's world. Everything about it is built of wonder ; you hold your breath, fearing to take your eyes away, lest the whole thing sink back into the earth from which it was raised by magic. It is hard to believe that this palace, a miniature Alhambra, is made of mere stone or that this courtyard con-

THE DONKEY OF GOD

tains flowers that grow in a world of men and machines. Even the cathedral seems unreal, in spite of its Norman sculptures, its three-storied bell-tower and its great bronze doors of the twelfth century.

Nor is there anything matter-of-fact about the pulpit, the most famous thing in Ravello. This huge balcony is borne by six stone lions; six twisted columns rise from their backs; the pulpit balances itself on this foundation—and every inch of marble is inlaid with running ribbons of mosaics. Mosaics fill the church with brilliance, sometimes in the form of patterns from a geometry, sometimes in biblical designs, one of which shows Jonah much bigger (and far stronger) than the weak and wistful whale.

The view from the old walls as you take your last look at the coast below, seemingly on another planet, is overpowering. You seem to be peering through the wrong end of a wizard's telescope, a telescope made of air.

The drive to Salerno is a long succession of beauties. The highway itself is a kind of miracle of road-building. Forty miles long, beginning at Castellamare, stretched along the Mediterranean, most of it is cut through the cliffs that line the coast. At times the road runs at dizzy levels; here it dips toward a picture-book village, there it rises towards new heig supported by arched viaducts five hundred feet above sea-level.

This is the country of large vineyards and small villages. Between Amalfi and Salerno half a dozen townlets make the

RAVELLO—SALERNO—PAESTUM

trip colourful : Cetara, dominated by its romantic watch-tower ; Maiori, with its fishing-smacks and its delicate spires ; Minori (Major and Minor, of course, meaning Greater and Lesser), with its old round fountain which is said to have a private water-nymph of its own ; Vietri sul Mare (on the sea), with its palms and pear-cactus, the fruit of which is called " Indian figs " and is relished by the natives ; Atrani, curved like a scimitar, with its jewel-box church where the rulers of Amalfi were elected and entombed when Amalfi was a powerful city of fifty thousand, governing colonies in Africa, and its word was law throughout the Mediterranean.

Salerno has shrunk in grandeur almost as much as Amalfi. From a great medieval city, it has become a small business centre. But its setting is still superb. It is fixed like a gold half-moon " where the mountains meet the sea " in its own Gulf of Salerno. The cornflower-blue waters lie at its feet ; its hem is fringed with emerald ferns and the great plumed century-plant ; it is crowned with a diadem of lemon and orange trees. Orange and lemon trees shine out everywhere along the Amalfi drive, but nowhere more brightly than here. And here, undisturbed by the modern world, is the cathedral whose bronze doors were made in Constantinople in the eleventh century ; and here lies Hildebrand, a carpenter's son who became Pope.

THE DONKEY OF GOD

Young Hildebrand worked in his father's shop, one of the busiest in Tuscany. He liked to watch the shavings curl under the knife; he was pleased with the smell of new-cut olive and cedar wood; he enjoyed fitting pegs into tables and legs into chairs as though they were building-toys. Most of all he liked making crosses, and as he grew older he began to carve the great crucifixes for the churches of Tuscany.

One day, as he sat smoothing a finished cross, he thought of him who was to be placed upon it and it seemed that he heard a voice speaking from the piece of wood.

" Hildebrand," said the voice, " I, too, was a carpenter's son. With wood and nails I began my life; with wood and nails my life was taken. But the end is not yet. Arise, follow me and do my work."

So Hildebrand knew he had been called. He left the carpenter's shop and entered a monastery. As a monk he brooded over the wickedness of his times, a wickedness which had affected and even corrupted Christianity. As he grew more religious he grew more ashamed that high positions in the Church could be bought like so much merchandise. He preached against this evil (called simony) and, by practising as he preached, Hildebrand became a power throughout Europe. It was he who was responsible for having the Pope elected by a College of Cardinals, not merely appointed or supported by some political ruler. Many opposed him, but

RAVELLO—SALERNO—PAESTUM

in the year 1073 he was elected Pope under the title of Gregory VII.

Now his enemies feared and fought him more than ever. Chief among them was the German Emperor Henry IV. In spite of Pope Gregory's orders, Henry appointed several bishops and allowed his officials to take money for favouring them. Gregory promptly deposed the Emperor's bishops and punished the officials. Henry replied by deposing Gregory and appointing a council of his own. The duel was on and the issue was clear: Gregory wanted to keep the State a part of the Church; Henry fought to make the Church dependent on the State. It was a fierce struggle, bitterly waged on both sides. Finally Henry's own people began to waver; his nobles turned against him, and the Church was, for the time being, the victor. The proud Henry was forced to humble himself. He and his grasping bishops were compelled to cross the Alps in the coldest mid-winter and beg forgiveness of Gregory who was in the Castle of Canossa. There, because of his haughtiness, the Emperor had to wait three days outside the gates, dressed as a penitent in nothing but a coarse shirt of sackcloth, praying and fasting in the snow. At the end of the third day he and his followers were admitted and pardoned. But, as soon as he was back in his own palace, Henry claimed the terms were too hard; he could not—or would not—fulfil them; and again he challenged Gregory.

THE DONKEY OF GOD

Appointing a Pope of his own, Henry once more declared war on Gregory and, this time aided by bought troops, entered the holy city of Rome. Gregory sent an appeal to Robert Guiscard, the captain of a large army of freebooters, and Guiscard's forty thousand forced Henry's soldiers to flee. But Gregory's friend turned out to be worse than his enemy. As soon as Henry was expelled, Guiscard's soldiers seized Rome for themselves. They plundered the town; private houses and palaces were robbed of their treasures; even the churches were attacked. The havoc was terrific. The damage preyed on Gregory's mind; the shock broke his heart. He retired to Salerno and, a year later, died there.

You will find the remains of the great reformer in the cathedral whose marble pulpit is so like the one at Amalfi. And in the cathedral facing the tomb of Gregory, by the irony of chance, are a set of columns stolen from Paestum by Robert Guiscard.

The road to Paestum is not wide nor imposing; the chief highway ends at Salerno. But, if it is less cultivated, it is more unusual. The antique world creeps back here; every foot of it recalls forgotten centuries. The olive trees help. The olive trees resemble nothing so much as ghosts of trees. And that is only natural since many are a hundred and more years old.

RAVELLO—SALERNO—PAESTUM

Some of them seem to have died and left only a part of their trunks standing, and from a mere fragment of bark new branches whisper of life everlasting. Others throw out arms like a frightened octopus and twist and try to turn themselves inside out. But, though no two olive trees have the same shape, all have the same grey-silver leaves dulled by the winds and thinned by time. In the moonlight, the trees seem to be hung with antique coins.

If you are looking for entertainment at Paestum you will be disappointed. Once a famous Greek settlement, then a Roman city, then a Moorish town, Paestum is now nothing except a small cluster of ruins. There is no sign of the statues and shrines that used to line its streets; except for scattered rough-hewn stones, there is scarcely a trace of the streets themselves. There is no longer a sea-wall with flags flying from its towers to announce the arrival of ships from Athens; you look out over deserted fields to an empty sea. Yet the remains of Paestum's three temples tell a silent story of its vanished greatness.

Two of the temples have been named (the temple of Neptune and the temple of Ceres) and the Doric columns of the first form one of the noblest pieces of architecture in the world. They seem built to stand for ever; built, one might say, not only of stone but of space. These three magnificent pieces of " frozen music " planned over two thousand years ago have

THE DONKEY OF GOD

outlived not only the race which worshipped in them but the gods they celebrated. And yet—

The next story is about this " and yet—." I said that two of the temples had been named. The third temple is a mystery. No one has ever found out its name, its age or the god to whom it was dedicated. The story that follows—which is supposed to have happened only a few years ago—tries to tell a little more about that particular temple, the town, and a boy who lived there.

THE TEMPLE-BOY

—AND CARRIED HIM TO THE NOBLEST CHAMBER IN HEAVEN

THE TEMPLE-BOY

LUCA was not like the other boys of Paestum. They were lusty fellows with black hair, keen eyes and a great fondness for games like " Strike-your-Neighbour," " Chase Me " and " Kings-and-Robbers." Luca's hair was pale, his eyes were weak and so was his back. As for games, the only one he could play was the game that began " I wish "—and that he played alone. When the other boys played " Follow-your-Leader " up and down the alleys, Luca would look after them longingly and walk to the ruined temples just outside of the village. There were three of them, the temple of Neptune which was the largest (for the old sea-town had been dedicated to the god of the sea), the temple of Ceres, and one temple so old that nobody knew its name. Even the schoolmasters were uncertain.

It was to this temple Luca always went during his childhood, and it was here that he came after his first day of the new term. It had been a hard day. He had been made uncomfortable by the rougher boys; the girls had teased him about his yellow hair; the schoolmaster had spoken sharply and had rapped him over the knuckles.

"You must pay closer attention," the schoolmaster had said. "You're not here to dream, but to study!"

Yet just when Luca should have been preparing his homework, he was doing the very thing the schoolmaster had forbidden. He was dreaming. He could scarcely help it. His head was heavy with large numbers and long words, with names he was told not to forget and dates he would never remember. Besides, the sun was just in the right place—not too high and not too hot—the smell of the acanthus was drowsy and the ferns made a soft mattress for his always tired back. He watched a grass-green lizard slither down a column, and then, motionless as a twig on a day with no wind, fall asleep in the sun. His eyes grew heavier, even as he studied an ant pulling a beetle ten times its size over pebbles that must have seemed great cliffs to the insect.

"If I were only strong!" Luca thought. "If I had three wishes, I would first wish I could lift any load in the world. Then I would wish—let me see—I would wish—"

But Luca's eyes had closed. Before he had time to complete his second wish he was as fast asleep as the lizard.

It was then he had the first of his peculiar dreams. He saw himself in the old temple just as he had fallen asleep; but the ground, instead of being covered with ferns, was lined with

THE TEMPLE-BOY

boards and crowded with desks. The place where the altar had stood was a low platform, and on this platform a group of stern-faced figures—most of them with beards—were staring at Luca. Their faces were strange, yet somehow familiar; in another moment Luca knew he was face to face with the ancient gods.

"What right has this unbeliever in our sacred haunts?" thundered one of them, rattling his sword so loudly that Luca knew at once it must be Mars.

"And dreaming! Here of all places!" rumbled the largest, longest-bearded one of the group, who Luca knew must be Jupiter, though he looked something like the schoolmaster. And this was strange because the schoolmaster was a thin, hairless man with a voice like a bad-tempered whistle.

"Don't you know it's against the rules?" questioned a voice like the tide coming in, a voice that belonged to Neptune. "Besides, why did you select this temple instead of mine to sleep in?"

"And don't you know," continued Jupiter, "that's enough to make any god angry! You shouldn't come here to dream, but to study!"

"Punishment! Punishment!" all the gods cried then. All except one. The rest were silent as this one stood up. The skin of a lion was flung over one shoulder, a knotted club was balanced on the other, and Luca knew it was Hercules.

THE DONKEY OF GOD

"One moment, your majesties," said Hercules, in a voice that was commanding though quiet. "This is my temple; and it is I who have the right to pass judgment. I have watched this lad for a long time—even as a child he sought these sacred stones. He is not an unbeliever; his heart has led him here. Many lives ago he was a temple-boy at this very altar; later he became my high-priest. I stood behind him then; I will support him now. Always have I been the god of the strong. But I do not forget my true servants, and now I shall be the guardian of the weak." As Hercules spoke, his face grew larger and larger, filling the temple. All the other voices were blotted out as he said, "Luca, rest easy. You are under my protection now."

The next day the pupils had to tell some experience that had happened to them lately. Some of the boys told about a visit to a large city or what they had done during the summer; the girls related how they had learned to cook *zucchini*—those extra-thin gourd-cucumbers—or take care of a baby-goat whose mother had died. Luca could think of nothing except his dream of yesterday. But he had not reached the end before he was stopped.

"That's not an experience," snapped the schoolmaster. "That's rubbish. In the first place, the temple you mention has never had a name. Not even the most renowned scholars know who was worshipped there. It is called the Basilica—write

THE TEMPLE-BOY

it down—B-a-s-i-l-i-c-a, which means—well, you wouldn't understand it anyway. Besides, the names you used are those of the Roman gods—and I can think of nothing more absurd than Roman gods speaking Italian in a Greek temple!" He snorted, as a penny-whistle might snort. "I shall not give you a good mark for to-day's work, Luca. No. You must learn to apply yourself. Use your eyes instead of your imagination. And don't let me have to speak to you again about this day-dreaming! Hercules indeed!"

The following term they had long history lessons. At the end of the month, the schoolmaster told them to write a composition on the history of their part of the country—"and mind you," he said, "be sure to get the facts—all the facts—and get them right!"

In his room at home Luca tried to get the facts in order. But names and dates kept tangling each other up; jumping into Luca's mind and, just as he was ready to put them on paper, jumping out again. He spent most of the afternoon breaking the points of two pencils and sharpening them, chewing one end after another. Three hours more of this and all he had for the afternoon's work was a small pile of crumpled paper and a headache. At five o'clock he got up, left the house, and went to his favourite place among the temples.

Once more he fell asleep near the altar and once more he forgot his troubles in a dream. This time it seemed that he was walking along the sea-shore. His pains had gone, his body felt strong, but otherwise he was the same Luca except for the fact that his clothing was quite different. Instead of the torn shirt and patched trousers, he was dressed in a white robe with a golden girdle; instead of his brother's worn-out jacket, a small cape of fine fleece was about his shoulders, and soft sandals of kid-skin were on the usually naked feet. He tried to think of the history-lesson, but his eyes were fixed on a lion-coloured cloud that seemed to shake in the windy skies. The cloud grew until it covered the heavens like a mantle, still rising and falling as though some one were running with it. Then Luca realised that the cloud actually was a cloak, and that it belonged to a god who was coming down to earth. As soon as he realised this, the god began speaking.

"Yes," said the voice which he knew was Hercules', "I have not forgotten. You are still under my care, my especial protection. See, you are clad in the dress you used to wear when you were my temple-boy over two thousand years ago. And now I will give you the gift of new eyes—the eyes of the gods when they want to look backward and forward in time. Look now—and you will see centuries roll back, one by one. You will not see me, but I will be with you. Look now—"

As the cloud disappeared, Luca found himself standing in the old temple without a name. It was deserted and in ruins just as he always saw it, with the grass-green lizards out-slid-

THE TEMPLE-BOY

ing the snakes one minute and standing stiller than a leaf the next.

Then the temple began to fill. Monuments were at the entrances, statues stood in every corner. But they did not stand there long. Men in a kind of armour Luca had never seen began dragging them away; marble columns were thrown down and carted off toward Salerno; a bull-necked leader hurried the workers who kept on crossing themselves. And Luca knew this was the wicked Robert Guiscard and he was destroying the temple to build up the cathedral in Salerno so he might be forgiven for his sins. Luca watched the scene until it faded. Then the centuries rolled backward in time and another scene took its place.

The view was the same—here were the three temples—but it was two hundred years earlier. Paestum was now a thriving seaport, the temple of Neptune was used as an early Christian church, and one of the Popes had sent a bishop for the growing town. Suddenly the city was full of strange bronze-coloured men, men who spoke a harsh tongue and held nothing sacred. There were thousands upon thousands of them, swarming in the streets like evil, murderous rats. They ransacked the shops; they tore down the crosses; cut through the crowds with curved swords; they spared no one. Luca knew he was witnessing the invasion of the Saracens, and when they had gone there was nothing left of Paestum except a river of blood

THE DONKEY OF GOD

and the three temples. They were the only things that did not fade as the scene blurred out.

Once more time turned back. The centuries flew swifter now, past the Popes, past the beginnings of the Christian faith. Now the pictures paused for a moment and Luca saw the Emperor Augustus dining under a great awning held up by trees of living roses while a banquet lasting eight hours was served. Each course was tendered by slaves in different costumes while the head butlers brought in such delicacies as sea-mice in honey, nightingales' tongues, a whole roast ox stuffed with sweet loaves inside of which were jewels, rare fruit powdered with pearl-dust, and a great pudding piled up to represent Vesuvius, with flames and fire-works coming out of the peak. He saw the cornflower-coloured sea turn red with fire from the real volcano and black with the cloud of ashes that followed. Then, as time continued to turn back, he saw the sea grow yellow with sails from Africa, saw the great Carthaginian generals come ashore with gold and promises, saw the heads of the town refuse to join the foreigners, saying, " We remain faithful to Rome."

Another hundred years flew back. Two hundred. Five hundred. Paestum was now Poseidonia, the city of Poseidon, which was Neptune's Greek name. Luca watched the stones of the three temples rise from the earth, mount to their proper places, fit themselves until they had formed great rows of columns,

THE TEMPLE-BOY

walls, half-open ceilings that framed the sky. Colours shone out of the statues; gold and enamel brightened every cornice; even the streets were paved in marble. Strange men and women gossiped, boys called to each other on their way to the amphitheatre, the priests chanted while the sacrifice was prepared—and Luca understood every word. He felt more at home in this forgotten Greek colony than in the town of his own times. He saw a boy of his very build putting sharp-smelling twigs on the altar-fire and when the boy turned toward Luca, he was not surprised to see his own face.

"Praise be to thee, Hercules," said the boy who was Luca many lives ago, "and bless the least of thy worshippers—" and bright sea-salt was thrown on the flames which sparkled like running jewels.

Then the smoke roared like a lion; it thickened and assumed the shape of a god. And the smoke replied, "The least worshipper will not be forgotten. My true servants will be remembered until the end of time, no matter how long time may run, nor whether it run forward or backward. I am the god of the strong; but I am also the guardian of the weak."

Then Luca woke and, for the time being, he felt strong in every fibre; he walked home with a firm step and eyes that were unaware of the dusk. He did not notice that the dews had fallen, that his body was damp, and that he was coughing more than usual.

THE DONKEY OF GOD

In his room he lit his two candle-ends and wrote down as much as he could remember. But when he brought it to class the schoolmaster was even less pleased than before.

" Do you call that history ? " he whistled in a thin pipe of anger. " Where are the dates ? How many miles is it from the temples in Paestum to the cathedral in Salerno ? In what direction was the wind blowing when the ships came from Africa ? You've left out everything important. Besides, you spelt two of the names wrong. And you should have named *all* the Caesars in the proper order. Facts ! Facts ! Will you *never* learn ! "

The rest of the term went by, but Luca missed most of it. His cough grew worse ; his back could scarcely carry his head. He was forbidden to work ; forbidden to attend school ; at last he was forbidden to leave his bed. That was the hardest of all, for it meant he could not visit his temple. He still dreamed, but his dreams were not as clear as they used to be.

At the beginning of the next term the schoolmaster came to see him.

" Luca," said the schoolmaster, and his voice was kindlier, like a steaming kettle promising tea. " Luca, since you can't

THE TEMPLE-BOY

have your lessons in school I'm going to send them—or a part of them—here. There's one subject I know you will like; and I hope to see you make better progress in it than in the others. It's the study of the stars, or, to put it simply, Elemental Astronomy."

The words did not seem particularly simple to Luca, but the idea excited him. To know about the stars—to learn their names, study their natures—! He could scarcely sleep. His pulse beat faster, his head was hot, his body light. He felt he could float away—and presently he did. Out of the window he drifted, lighter than the air which carried him, soaring, soaring until he was miles above the world.

Paestum was only a faint cluster of lights now; then it dwindled to one twinkling spark; then the spark went out. Now all the bright earth seemed smaller than a lamp, a candle-end, a glowworm. Then it, too, flickered and went out. There was nothing underneath Luca now except darkness.

But overhead all was brilliance. As the lights of earth grew dimmer, the lights of heaven grew greater. The constellations —those shining groups—filled in the spaces between their separate stars and took their true shapes. Luca could recognise them now. Here was the Water-Carrier, every inch of him formed of moons and planets, skimming the Milky Way with the Dipper made of seven stars. Here was that radiant menagerie, the Whale and the Sea-Serpent, the Swan and the Dragon, the Lion and the Bull, the Little Bear and the Great Bear, as well as their Keeper whose glory is the brightest star of the summer sky. Here came shining Perseus, the mighty, astride of The Winged Horse and there was the Ram which had escaped from the heavenly Herdsman. It seemed to Luca that the Ram, whose tail was a comet and whose horns were tipped with sharp-pointed stars, was coming straight at him, and for a moment he longed for the earth.

Then he heard a voice echoing from the furthest heavens and fear left him.

" Because you could not come to my temple upon earth," sang the starshine, " I have brought you to my temple in the skies. A god does not forget the least of his worshippers. I said you would be remembered until the end of time, no matter how long time might run, and now my promise is about to be fulfilled. You have loved the gods; therefore you shall live among them. Come."

And Hercules lifted Luca upon his glittering shoulders and carried him to the noblest chamber in heaven.

Next week the schoolmaster showed his pupils a new star. " These things have appeared before," said the schoolmaster, " and, though unusual, they are not miraculous. Such phenomena—write it down—p-h-e-n-o-m-e-n-a—were observed by the ancients who often saw heavenly bodies appear suddenly

THE TEMPLE-BOY

and slowly fade away. The ancients, however, were superstitious and believed a new star meant that the gods had found a new favourite and had fixed a special place for him. To-day we know that such ideas are held only by foolish folk and that such an occurrence may be explained by—write these words down—meteors . . . comets . . . nebulae . . . "

Meanwhile, somewhere between Neptune and Hercules, Luca continued to shine.

THE HILL-TOWNS — 1

ORVIETO — PERUGIA — ASSISI

ASSISI

ORVIETO—PERUGIA—ASSISI

HOW true, I have been asked, is this story of the temple-boy? I must confess that it is so long since I watched the lizards scuttling up the pillars that I can scarcely tell where fact ends and fiction begins. But I do know that the stones of the three temples are still standing at Paestum, that the basilica is still without a name, and that the columns which Luca saw being dragged away toward Salerno are part of the cathedral of that town. The ending—the transformation of Luca into a star—may be less convincing. But let me remind the reader that a new star, one of the furthest planets, was discovered beyond Mercury just a few years ago. At first the great astronomers refused to believe it, but finally they admitted it was not only a genuine star but an important one. Like the basilica, it had no name and, after many suggestions, they gave it one of their own—Pluto they called it. Yet, in spite of the learned astronomers, I have my private opinion. I like to believe it is Luca.

In any case, it shines.

THE DONKEY·OF GOD

But we must be on our way. There are, I should add, many ways. One of them runs south and brings us to the extreme tip of Italy, the large toe on the map, and so to Sicily. But Sicily, being a world in itself, deserves at least a book to itself. The other road runs north, as far north as you want to go. All roads, they say, lead to Rome ; and this road is no exception. But we will not stop there now. I am keeping Rome for a climax, and there is much to be seen in the meanwhile, especially in the fabled hill-towns.

The hill-towns stretch between Rome and Florence ; you can cover the distance in a single day. And you can spend years on the way without exhausting the wonders of such towns as Orvieto, Perugia, Assisi, Gubbio, Siena, San Gimignano. Go where you will, stay where you will, one village is lovelier than the other ; each town has its separate and yet related story ; every inch is colourful in this " garden of the world." The words Byron wrote to Italy a century ago are true to-day :

> Thy very weeds are beautiful, thy waste
> More rich than other clime's fertility ;
> Thy wreck a glory, and thy ruin graced
> With an immaculate charm which cannot be defaced.

ORVIETO—PERUGIA—ASSISI

Byron's words are especially true of the hill-towns, and these are best approached by way of Orvieto.

According to the historians, Orvieto is much older than Rome; it was one of the twelve ancient capitals of perished Etruria, and the jewels and vases found in the Etruscan tombs show how important the city must have been even in pre-Roman days. But, as you approach the town, you forget all your history; the mere look of it takes facts and figures as well as your breath away. Orvieto, which can be seen miles away, rises clear off the earth; the entire city stands on a platform of rock, the sides of which are straight as a cliff. It is as if Nature had thrown up an immense natural fort in the midst of a plain and it is no wonder that Orvieto became both a stronghold and a place of refuge.

Higher and higher the walls of the city tower. The battlements made by man can hardly be distinguished from those made by the rock; the medieval turrets frown on the intruder. At last the summit is mounted; the huge gate opens and, suddenly, you are back in the Middle Ages and in front of another miracle in stone, the great Orvieto cathedral.

The cathedral of Orvieto is, according to the authorities, one of man's most remarkable efforts. Outside and inside it is a jewel-box on a colossal scale: the front of it glittering with many-coloured marble and gem-like mosaics; its lacy rose-window, more like a chiselled marigold than a rose; its columns

THE DONKEY OF GOD

that could be studied for days, each with a different set of legends; the interior passing beyond description. Begun in the year 1285 it makes our modern structures look short-lived and gaudy. The reliefs on the façade (or front) are a dozen story-books cut in stone; fables, biblical tales and lessons spread themselves out like branches of a tree. One pilaster (or column) is covered with a running vine in the curves of which can be seen the beginnings of the world and the creation of man. Another tells the history of Jesus in twenty intertwined scenes. A third shows Abraham and his descendants. The fourth—and the finest—pictures the resurrection and last judgment. This theme is extended to the interior where the frescoes by Fra Angelico and Signorelli brilliantly contrast hell and heaven. Only in the cemetery at Pisa will you see more graphic and more gripping murals.

Besides the cathedral—and the guide will not let you forget the delicately carved marble altars—there are the Etruscan tombs and the mysterious well of San Patrizio. This curious structure, begun in 1527 and finished thirteen years later, is a remarkable engineering work—especially when one considers the crude machinery of the times. It is a tower rather than a well, a tower that works its way into the earth instead of rising from it, going down two hundred feet through solid rock. There are two separate stair-cases; one for the people to descend, one for the water-carriers to carry up their burdens without interfering with each other. The plan of the town

ORVIETO — PERUGIA — ASSISI

is like that of the well. There are the corkscrew alleys, the streets that look as though they had been cut through the walls with a thin knife, and the remains of various palaces.

Before you finish travelling in Italy, you will tire of hearing about the ancient walls, watch-towers and castles that stand out like exclamation-points in the landscape. But the palace at which you stop in Orvieto is like no other. If you stop in Orvieto at all, you will stop there, for it is now the town's chief hotel. There is a courtyard more romantic than most romances and a private banquet-hall in which, if the hotel is not too crowded, your supper is served before an open fire and you wait (alas, in vain!) for the appearance of the garlanded boar's head and an assortment of wandering troubadours. Still, there is a sight that is equally memorable and it happens twice a week. I shall never forget it.

I had gone to sleep in a room about the size of a battlefield and had slept as soundly as though machines and motorcars had never been invented. In fact, I had dreamed a dream of an earlier age and when I waked I was still living in another century. Or was it a dream? Thin edges of light, fingering their way through the tall shutters, showed nothing of the modern world. A muffled bell began to speak in the tones of the Middle Ages and morning began to stir. There was a noise in the courtyard—a noise that would tell me whether I was still dreaming or merely lost in time. The courtyard was still

THE DONKEY OF GOD

grey; but it was coming alive with misty figures. Many of them were on horseback, and, though I could not see their armour, I could hear the clatter of metal. Commanding voices called, knights dismounted, canopies sprang up, horses champed at their jousting-bits, the air grew tense with activity. I knew the tournament was about to begin and that, somehow, I had slipped back into the fifteenth century. I leaned on the window-sill; it was cold and hard and the edge of it hurt my hand. No; I was not asleep.

Then daylight came quickly and my eyes corrected my ears. The clatter of metal turned out to be the rattle of pots and pans; the canopies were the covers for common booths; the commanding voices were those of farmers and small tradesmen. In a twinkling the tournament became a market-place and the only contests were those between buyer and seller. Yet the actual scene was as fascinating as the one created by the imagination. The mad mixture of costumes, colours, men and merchandise made it look something like a fair and something like a festival. I longed for some painter to reproduce this old man with his two very young calves to which he was talking as though they were spoiled children. I wanted some one to immortalise this strapping peasant-woman with her six or eight live hens tied together and which she unconcernedly carried about her neck like a living, loudly protesting feather-boa; and this enormous dame, who looked as if she were made

ORVIETO — PERUGIA — ASSISI

of a mountain of dough, sitting so silently behind her loaves of bread that she seemed part of her own baking; and this brisk little merchant, springing among his boxes of toys as though after winding up the clock-work trains, he had wound himself up. But it was useless to wish for an artist to do justice to market-day in that courtyard; it would require the genius of a Rembrandt, the skill of a jeweller, the humour of a Mark Twain and the beauty of an old ballad all blended into one. ... We went on toward Perugia.

Before leaving Orvieto we heard the legend of the Cardinal and his courier. There was, it seems, a Cardinal who was extremely fond of the good things in life. He insisted that he must have pleasant things about him to taste, touch and observe. Since he had to travel a great deal, he had, in his employ, a courier who went before him to investigate and report on the towns which the Cardinal was to visit. The courier was always on the look-out for three things: good food, good wine and beautiful women. And wherever he found one of the three he would write on the town wall the Latin word " *Est* " (" It is "), meaning " This is the place." Sometimes the food was good, sometimes the women were fair, sometimes the wine was excellent; but " never the three together." Often, indeed, he had to pass half a dozen villages, for the Cardinal was very particular. But, so runs the tale, when the courier came to the outskirts of Orvieto he could scarcely express himself for

THE DONKEY OF GOD

delight. The food at the inns was rich and lavish; the women were lovely; and as for the wonderful wine—! A few days later when the Cardinal's retinue arrived, they saw written on the town wall in great sprawling letters: " *Est ! Est ! ! Est ! ! !* "

That which so delighted the courier found even more favour with the Cardinal. He never left the town; he lived and died there the happiest of mortals. . . . Such, at least, is the legend. This much is undisputed fact: Orvieto still boasts beautiful daughters; its food is famous; and the sweet wine from the neighbouring Montefiaschone (The Hill of Flasks) is proudly labelled " *Est ! Est ! ! Est ! ! !* "

At Perugia you are in the centre of three civilisations: the ancient Etruscan, the Roman, and the Medieval. The very town gates show how one was built on the other; in every street the past is more powerful than the present. Like Orvieto, Perugia is set on a high plateau and its majestic situation has given it the title " Empress of the Umbrian plain." Churches grow thick as olives here; bastions and towers plant themselves on their own rocks; every cathedral is an art gallery.

Mention of an art gallery reminds me of the fact that the names of Italian painters are very rarely their own names. For

ORVIETO — PERUGIA — ASSISI

example, Perugia became the home of a certain Pietro Vannucci whose paintings became so celebrated that the name Vannucci was discarded and he became known as *Perugino,* " the one from Perugia." The real name of *Tintoretto* was Jacopo Rubusti and he was nicknamed Tintoretto il Furioso (The Fast and Furious Dyer) because his father was a dyer of cloth and because of the high speed at which he worked. *Andrea del Sarto* signified Andrea (or Andrew) the Son of the Tailor. Paolo di Dono was called *Paolo Uccello* because he loved to put birds (*uccelli*) in his paintings. The *Pisanos,* that famous family of sculptors, medallists, and workers in bronze, were so called because they came from Pisa. The celebrated *Pinturicchio* (The Noble Painter) was a native of Perugia and was born humble Bernardino di Betto. *Fra Angelico* (The Angelic Brother) was really Giovanni da Fiesole (Fiesole being a suburb of Florence); even during his life-time his associates gave him the title of Beato, or the Blessed, because of the beatific quality of his work. It is said that he never took up pencil or brush without asking the help of Heaven and that he never painted the Saviour except on his knees.

The painter Perugino is seen at his best, naturally enough, in his own town, especially in the series of decorations in the Collegio del Cambio which used to be Perugia's Stock Exchange or Chamber of Commerce. I have no intention of describing those remarkable frescoes; they must be seen to be

THE DONKEY OF GOD

appreciated—if mere seeing can appreciate them. Nor will I attempt to picture the great piazza in the centre of the town, nor the Palazzo Communale, which is a town hall, a picture-gallery and an example of the purest Gothic palace all in one. Nor will I point out the fine old fountains, particularly the one by the Pisano family, nor the various churches—especially the imposing church of San Pietro—most of which are treasure-houses. The guides will do that.

Mention of the Etruscans—and every guide, textbook and advertisement of the Royal University for Foreigners will be sure to mention them—reminds me that one of the most interesting things in the neighbourhood of Perugia is not in Perugia itself, but lies two leisurely miles outside of its imposing walls. Along the timeless road to Assisi, where the olive trees assume the weirdest shapes, lies the tomb of the Volumnii. History refuses to say just how the Volumnii lived but that they were an important family-group is evident from this huge Etruscan vault. Although this is at least two thousand years old, it was discovered less than one hundred years ago, and it is one of the few perfect things of its kind. You go down a long flight of steps to find the entrance; and there, under the crust of the earth, lies this mysterious set of chambers. In the centre is a square cavern; nine smaller rooms open into it; the entire subterranean building is carved out of the underground rock. All is as it was in the remote era of 400 B.C.

ORVIETO—PERUGIA—ASSISI

—urns, marble coffins, Medusa's heads, uncanny symbols of death, lie in their appointed places. But though they tell us something, they cannot tell us all. Nor do the inscriptions help us. The words are there—the letters still clear in the stone—but they are part of a language no one can completely understand.

The very name of Assisi suggests Saint Francis; it is difficult to think of one without the other. But Assisi was a lordly town, commanding a view of the vast Umbrian plain, long before it became a popular shrine to the poverty-loving saint. In fact it was one of the most pleasure-seeking of the gay cities, and, before Francis became a monk, he was the gayest of gay blades. But that is another story—one that is coming.

To-day everything about Assisi is devoted to the saint. The monastery with the church of San Francesco is a huge memorial in his honour; every inch of the vestibules, the vaulted ceilings, the walls of the upper church, the chapels are crowded with legends that glorify him. The church itself is a mass of interwoven designs; Simone Martine of Siena and Giotto of Florence came here with their pupils to picture the visions and miracles of the mystic whose love for " the least of them " extended to " all things both great and small."

Assisi is, as you can imagine, a holy city. It is not only sacred to Saint Francis but to Saint Clara, a noblewoman of Assisi who gave up wealth and position to become his disciple.

THE DONKEY OF GOD

Here is the "Porziuncola," where the first members of the Franciscan order gathered to hear him. Here is the tiny chapel to which come pilgrims from all over the world; here is the cell (now lavishly decorated) where the austere saint died.

Most of the legends about Francis have been told and retold. (In another chapter, I may repeat one or two of them.) But there is one which has never been recorded—for the very good reason that it never existed until it came to me. Part of it came in a dream, the rest of it fitted in the first time I saw a certain diminutive donkey staggering under a huge load. The donkey wasn't much bigger than a large dog, but he was pulling a whole family of Italians, to say nothing of the household goods and a few barrels of olive oil. He trudged on uncomplainingly, but his eyes told more than most books. Later, I bought him and brought him to America. He stood the ocean trip well and now he is the boon companion of the cows and the collies on our Adirondack acres. It was in his eyes, as well as in Assisi, that I found the story of "The Donkey of God."

THE DONKEY OF GOD

HG

SO THE ARCHANGEL MICHAEL CALLED ALL THE ANIMALS

THE DONKEY OF GOD

YOU must know that, at the time of this story, Italy was not one country as she is to-day. Italy was divided into many provinces, each of them jealous of the other. There was not even a united feeling within the provinces themselves. In the Middle Ages every city had its own government, and every city hated its neighbour. Milan fought with Mantua ; Florence despised Siena and spoke of its citizens as " the treacherous Sienese "; Pisa sneered at Florence, there being continual conflict between the proud Pisans " already powerful when the ancient Greeks struggled beneath the walls of Troy " and " the upstart Florentines " ; Assisi and Perugia always had been at war with each other.

Assisi claimed to be the oldest of the hill-towns. It boasted of tombs that were even older than the temple-ruins ; its vine-terraced slopes grew the richest grapes and the juiciest olives. More important from the point of view of the generals of Assisi, those slopes commanded a view of the Umbrian valley and no enemy could approach without being seen from a great

THE DONKEY OF GOD

distance. Thus prepared and fortified, Assisi was a happy place. It was even a merry one. Its merchants were wealthy, its churches were richly decorated, its young people were dressed as though life were one long carnival.

Of all the gay youths none was as richly costumed as Francis. His father was a cloth-merchant and Francis was his favourite son. No wonder his horse was the swiftest, his cap-feather the longest, his armour the handsomest, and his eyes the most impudent in Assisi. No one danced more wildly in the festival masquerades; no one swung a lute so gallantly or composed a livelier serenade; no one shook his fist more patriotically than Francis at the towers of Perugia. When, after an uncomfortable peace, the neighbouring cities threatened a new war, no one was quicker to call for action than the bold son of the cloth-merchant.

" Let us not wait until Perugia comes out against us," cried Francis. " Let us carry the war into her own fields, against her own gates. Let our swords break down her pride; let torches lay waste the old enemy. On to Perugia ! "

A little past midnight, after the moon had gone down, the army from Assisi set out to surprise the foe. But the Perugians must have had the same idea, for that night the Umbrian plain held two armies marching against each other. It was still dark when they met. The surprise was complete and all plans of orderly battle vanished with the first blow. They fought reck-

THE DONKEY OF GOD

lessly in a blackness lit only by torches suddenly lifted, suddenly dashed out. The quiet plain was shocked from its nightly peace to a hideous awaking. Arrows and spear-throwing machines were useless; it was short range fighting. Shield and sword, mace and dagger rang against each other in utter confusion.

With the first streak of dawn the fight came to an end. The scene was horrible beyond description. Each army had killed more of its own men than the enemy's. What was left of the Perugians was a battered remnant of soldiers; the champions of Assisi were too worn to continue. Without another blow, without a word of hate, the remainder of the two armies turned toward their towns. No one had a boast left to utter. It was a broken army that returned to Assisi in a dull, red dawn. The stoutest of the old horsemen felt sick.

None felt sicker than Francis. He had seen things that turned his ideas upside down. He had seen a man lying dead —not beautifully dead like an image on a stone-coffin, but deformedly, unspeakably dead—dead at his feet. His encrusted armour was foul with blood—blood that, a few hours ago, had flowed in veins as happy as his—there was blood on his hands. His heart felt as though an unseen dagger had run through it. With the dawn something new had dawned in Francis, something that would not die.

For weeks he lay tossing in a high fever. The doctors could

THE DONKEY OF GOD

do nothing to make him rest. Francis would start from a short sleep, call out, and lie awake the rest of the night, crying things that no one could understand. He was wasting away; his condition seemed hopeless. On the fortieth day, after the doctors had shaken their heads and gone, Francis got up. No one saw him go. He walked out of the house at dawn as softly as the light that showed him the way. Assisi was just awaking as he passed through the crooked streets and out of the town.

It was a different Francis that wandered, silently and alone, past the Umbrian plain. The rich suit had been exchanged for a coarse brown frock; instead of a sword he carried a wooden staff; there were no ornaments on his sleeves, no feathers on his hat—even the hat was gone. The impudent look had vanished from his eyes, the lines of boastfulness had left his lips. The face of Francis had grown long and finely cut; the eyes looked *through* things, not merely at them; a light seemed to be upon his brow.

Forty more days Francis wandered. He crossed valleys and climbed mountains; now in shaded woods, now in sun-baked marshes, making his way without a chart. He journeyed through Orvieto and Rome as in a dream. At the end of the fortieth day he came to the sea. Still following some inner guide, he took a passage on a boat and landed on the island of Sardinia. He had no plan, but somehow he knew that he must work out his cure in this primitive place.

THE DONKEY OF GOD

Here, far from the frivolous life of his past, he learned to live. Poorer than the poorest peasant, he was grateful for the common *frue*, or sour milk, and he who had been used to the rarest and most delicate dishes considered an occasional bowl of fresh cheese, which the natives called *ricotta*, a great treat. He did not indulge himself often in this, nor, for that matter, in anything else; his little hut was the humblest on an island where everything was scanty.

Little by little Francis' health returned; his step grew more vigorous, and he became himself again. But it was another self that now saw grandeur in the lowly and good in everything. He preferred the simple customs and dignity of the poor Sardinians to the hot carelessness of his one-time companions. But, though he visited the peasants every evening, he spent most of his time alone. He learned to know the animals of the island and was trusted by them. He became so familiar a sight that even the shy mouflon, a sort of wild sheep, let him walk among them, stroking their long coats. He understood their ways; he began to understand their speech.

One day as he was walking among the ruins of monuments as old as the stone-age, he noticed he had gone farther than usual and was straying in a circle of queer structures that the natives called " Fairy Houses." He smiled as he thought of the fear the peasants had of these stone-chambers and the superstition that any one resting within the circle would

THE DONKEY OF GOD

" dream true." He noticed a donkey standing in the shade of a stunted tree, but it did not appear in the least astonished to see him. Now that he observed it closer, he could not remember ever having seen a donkey so small. It was no larger than a large dog, a sheep-dog with unusually long ears. Its ankles were more delicate than a deer's and the eyes had a speaking softness. But the most peculiar feature was revealed to Francis only when he stood close. The colour was a soft pigeon-grey without a spot except for one distinguishing mark : a pattern made by two intersecting lines of black, one line running down the back from head to tail, the other line running across the shoulders. Presently, Francis noticed that the animal was speaking to him and he was aware that he understood it.

" Tell me, my good man," it was saying, " for I can see you are good, is there no justice in creation ? Isn't it bad enough that we donkeys have to carry every sort of burden—twice as much as the much larger horse—without also being a joke among men and animals ? Is that just ? And if that were not enough, why should we be made still more foolish by having to wear such a disfiguring pattern on our back ? Can you answer that ? "

To his surprise, Francis heard himself replying to the little donkey as if he were a priest and it were one of his flock.

" Yes, my daughter, I think I can. There is a justice in all things, though we cannot see it at once. We must wait until the pattern is completed before we judge any of its parts. In your case the answer is easier than most, for you are the donkey of God."

" The donkey of God? " asked the little animal.

" Surely," replied Francis, amazed at the way he was talking, but keeping on in an even voice. " If you do not know your own story, I will tell it to you."

And Francis, who had never seen the creature before, and who certainly had never thought of its origin, heard himself telling this strange legend:

It was the morning of the Sixth Day. God had spent the First Day inventing Light. Then, seeing that continual light would be too cruel on the eyes, He made Darkness for relief. On the Second Day God had designed the seas and had put a clear border of sky about them to prevent the waters from overflowing. On the Third Day, being dissatisfied with the emptiness of a world of water, He had gathered the waters in one place and had put dry land carefully among the seas. He called the dry land Earth and liked it much better, especially after He had caused green things to grow and had planned fruit to come after the flower. He had told Himself

THE DONKEY OF GOD

it was good. On the Fourth Day God had looked at the widespread Heaven and realised it needed something. So He had put lights in it: a great gold light to rule the day, and a soft silver one to rule the night, and a lot of lesser lights to decorate the evening. And once more He had been pleased. On the Fifth Day He decided He wanted more motion and sound in the universe. So He had filled the waters with whales and minnows and the air with insects and eagles. He had smiled when the first whale, that island afloat, had blown his first spout, and His great heart had tightened when the lark, hoping to reach heaven, sang his first song.

And now it was the Sixth Day. The earth, God saw, needed life no less than the sea and sky. So early in the morning He began making animals. First He made small simple ones: the snake and the snail, the mouse and the mole, rat and rabbit, cat and dog, lamb and wolf, goat, mink, fox, hedge-hog, beaver, woodchuck and a hundred others, each after his kind. Then, watching them leap or crawl or dig or prowl, He tried the same design on an ever-growing scale. It was then He made donkey and deer, horse and cattle, lion and tiger, bear, buffalo, elk, the great apes, the giant lizards, the mammoths like mountains on the move. Then God, out of the humour of His heart, indulged Himself in a few experiments. He made the giraffe with his feet in the mud, his long neck lost in the leaves, and his silly head trying to scrape the stars. He tied a bird and a

THE DONKEY OF GOD

snake together and made the ostrich. He took a lump of clay, shaped it, unshaped it, dug His thumb twice into it and threw it away—and that was the camel. He thought of a hill-side with a tiny tail and nose-arm-fingers in one long trunk—and thus the elephant was made. He took some river-mud, breathed on it, changed His mind, saying, " No animal that looked like that would want to live "—and it was the hippopotamus. When He saw these absurd shapes strut about, He laughed so long that the stars began to fall from their places—some of them are still so loose that they tremble in the sky—and, for a while, He did nothing at all.

But since He was God, He could not stop creating. So in the afternoon He looked at everything and said, " It is good." After a little while He added, " But it could be better. It lacks something."

All afternoon He sat pondering among the clouds. At last toward evening, He said, " It is not enough like Me. I will take the very best soil from the earth, for this will be an earth-creature. I will mix it with water so he need not be afraid of the sea. I will knead it with air so he can trust himself in any element and even fly if he wishes. I will then put a spark of Myself deep in him so he may be God-like. And it will be Man."

When the animals heard this they began arguing with God.

" Consider, O Lord," said the lion in his gentlest, most per-

THE DONKEY OF GOD

suasive roar. He was already known as the king of beasts, so he spoke first. " Consider, O Lord, before You breathe life into the creature. If You make him of the elements, he will be master not only of them, but of us all."

" Yes," said the elephant with a gruff simplicity, " such an animal as Man will do no labour at all. He'll say he's not made for it, and we'll have to do his work for him."

" Not that we mind, Lord," hissed the serpent with false meekness. " But if You put Your spark in him, he'll think he's divine. And after he's mastered us—not that *we* mind—he'll try to master what created him. And then—"

" And then," said God in the still small voice which was more terrible than thunder, " he will be part of Me again. Meanwhile, I have no need of advice from My own creations."

And so He made Man.

You are wondering, I see, what had become of the donkey. Up to now he had done nothing but listen and mind his own affairs. While the others were arguing with God or grumbling among themselves, the donkey calmly went on eating rose-leaves and lettuces and growing lovelier every minute. Perhaps I should have told you that he had been born the most perfect of four-footed creatures. He was very much like the donkeys of to-day except that his colour was softer, his eyes more tender, his ankles even more graceful—and, at that time, the long ears of his great-great-grandchildren did not disfigure

THE DONKEY OF GOD

his head. Instead of the grotesque flapping sails of the donkey of to-day, the original donkey had two of the finest, most perfectly shaped ears you can imagine. They were like those of a dainty fox, only smaller, and so wax-like that you could half see through them. Everything satisfied him; he feared nothing; the world was good. So he continued to munch lettuces and rose-leaves.

The donkey was so busy eating—it was at the beautiful beginning of things when there were no worms in the lettuces nor thorns on the roses—that he did not see God make the first man. Nor did he see Him, late in the night, creating the first woman. The next morning—it was Sunday—the other animals told him about it and said the man-animal was called Adam and the woman-animal was called Eve. A little tired of doing nothing but eating, the donkey joined the other beasts and peered into the garden where the two newest-born creatures were sitting. When he saw them he burst into the loudest and most ridiculous laugh on earth. It was like no sound that had ever been made; it was the first wild, weird, astonishing bray. To-day only the smallest echoes are in the throat of all the donkeys, but then it rang so fiercely against the skies that it almost threw the fixed stars out of their courses.

"Ho-hee-haw!" screamed the donkey. "It is *too* funny! *Such* animals! They're made all wrong! No hide! No hoofs! Not even a tail! And so pink—so *naked*! God must have meant

THE DONKEY OF GOD

to put a coat of fleece on them and forgot it! Ho-hee-*haw*!"

Eve, frightened by the screaming and screeching, ran into the woods. Adam sprang to his feet.

"And look!" the donkey brayed in a still ruder laugh, while the other beasts roared and cackled and barked. "Look! The she-man runs on her hind legs! She doesn't even know how to walk! Ho-ho—hee—haw—hee—HAW!"

This was too much for Adam. He ran over to the donkey and grasped him by the ears. The donkey tried to pull himself free, but Adam held fast. As he tugged and Adam tightened, his ears began to stretch, grow long, longer. . . . And while they were pulling. God suddenly appeared.

Said the Lord, "Because you have spoiled My day of rest and because you have made fun of My creation you shall be punished. Because you saw fit to laugh at your betters, you shall never cease from laughing. But no one will listen with joy; your voice will be a mockery by day and a horror by night. The louder you laugh, the longer will you be despised. You shall serve man and be subject to him all the days of your life. Other animals shall serve him also: the horse, the cow, the elephant and the dog. But, unlike them, you shall work for man without winning his love. Unlike them, you shall resist him foolishly, and he shall beat you for it. You who are the most comely of My creatures shall be the most comic. Instead of roses you shall feed on thorns and thistles. You shall

THE DONKEY OF GOD

have a rope for a tail. And your ears shall remain long."

So it was decreed. And so it turned out. When Adam and Eve were forced to leave the Garden and go to work, the donkey went with them. Adam rode on the horse, the dog trotted at Eve's side, but it was the donkey who carried the tools, the spinning-wheel and all the household machinery. Throughout Adam's life the donkey was reminded of the saying about laughing last instead of first. Sometimes he was ashamed and dropped his long ears like a lop-eared rabbit; sometimes his pride came back and he refused to take another step. At such times Adam beat him and the donkey remembered the Lord's prophecy. He wondered how long the burdens would be piled upon him.

After Adam died the donkey thought things would go easier, but he soon realised his hardships were only beginning. He belonged, he discovered, not to one man but to all men. Cain, the brutal son of Adam, broke him to harness and made him drag a heavy plough. When Noah built the ark the donkey carried more timber than the elephant, but no one praised him for it. Forty days and forty nights the floating menagerie breasted the flood, and every day and most of the nights the other animals jeered and mocked him. He knew now what it was to be laughed at. And when the windows of heaven were closed and the fountains of the flood went back into the heart of the sea, the donkey walked the earth again with meek eyes

THE DONKEY OF GOD

and bowed head. From that time on he swore to serve man faithfully and ask no reward.

At the building of Babel, the donkey was there, working willingly, although he knew no tower built by hands would ever reach Heaven. After the city was deserted, the donkey helped Abraham with his flocks, and carried for Isaac, and wandered with Jacob. So, through Bible times, the donkey remained loyal to his masters. He brought Joseph and his twelve brothers together; he dragged bricks for the Hebrews during their long slavery in Egypt; he crossed the Red Sea with Moses; he was beaten for trying to save the wizard Balaam; he entered Canaan with Joshua.

He worked; he wandered; he did not die.

Years passed; centuries vanished. The donkey was in Palestine. His master was a carpenter in the little town of Nazareth, a good master by the name of Joseph, though far different from the Joseph who had become a ruler in the land of Egypt. He had worked for him a long time, and he had served his owner well. A few years ago, when Joseph and his wife Mary were on their wanderings, the little donkey carried them everywhere without complaining. They were terribly poor and innkeepers had no room for them. The donkey trudged on, carrying his load that seemed to grow heavier with each step. For a long day and a longer night, he plodded toward the distant haven, never stopping or stumbling till he brought them to the little

THE DONKEY OF GOD

town of Bethlehem. That night, in a cattle-stall, Mary's child had been born.

The donkey obeyed his master, but he worshipped his master's small son. The child was not only beautiful, but even as perfect as he seemed to his mother. Goodness shone from his eyes; miracles, they said, flowed from his hands. The donkey believed it, for he had seen one performed.

Once, when playing with some other children in the streets of Nazareth, the carpenter's son picked up some clay from the gutter and kneaded it into a shape. His companions gathered around to watch him.

" Good," said Simon, " let's all do it. What shall we model ? "

" Let's make horses," cried Zadoc, the son of the priest. " When I grow up I'm going to have six horses of my own— two white ones, two black ones and two horses with many-coloured coats."

" Stupid ! " said Azor, the broom-maker's child. " There are no horses with many-coloured coats. Besides, horses are too hard to model. Let's make pigeons."

So they started to make pigeons of clay. After a while Zadoc called out, " I've made seven. How many have the rest of you ? "

" Five," said Zithri, the beggar's boy.

" Four," said Simon.

" Three," said Azor.

" Two," said Jesus, who was the carpenter's son.

THE DONKEY OF GOD

" Only two ! " sneered Zadoc. " And not even good ones. Mine look much more like pigeons than yours ! "

" You are right," said Jesus and he tossed his aside. But though the clay pigeons were thrown, they did not fall to the ground. Instead, they hung in the air, spread wings and flew away.

The other children stared for a moment and then grew angry. " He's playing tricks on us ! " cried Zadoc, son of the priest. " Let's play a trick on him ! " The others joined Zadoc and soon they had tied the little Jesus tightly. The cord bit deep into his wrists but he did not cry.

" He's just making believe he's brave," said Zadoc. " He acts as if he were a king."

" All right," jeered Azor. " Let him be king."

" I'll get him a crown," shouted Zithri.

They pulled down part of a withered rose-tree and twisted two small branches into a crown. They pressed this upon his forehead and cried, " King Jesus ! Hail to King Jesus ! " Then they ran away laughing, while tears stood in the eyes of the carpenter's son.

The donkey had seen it all, had seen that the hands of Jesus were still tied and that the child could not remove the crown of thorns. Then he nuzzled his soft nose along the child's shoulder, raised his head and, though the thorns stabbed his lips, lifted the piercing weight from Jesus' fore-

THE DONKEY OF GOD

head. He tugged at the cords till he freed the child's hands; then he carried him home.

More years passed. Jesus had gone away. Though the donkey did not know it, the carpenter's son had grown from childhood to manhood, had travelled and studied, had healed the sick, restored eyesight to the blind, cast out devils, had suffered untold hardships. But now the moment had come; Jesus was to enter Jerusalem in triumph.

It was a tremendous moment; one that must be celebrated in the proper manner. Naturally, Jesus could not enter the queen-city of Palestine on foot; he must ride, they said, on a charger worthy of the event. So the Archangel Michael called all the animals before Jesus that they might plead their case.

" Choose me," said the lion. " I am king of the beasts; you are a king among men. Men respect royalty—but only when they recognise it! When the people of Jerusalem see you riding on my back, they will know you are of noble blood and they will bow down and fear you. With me as your mascot, they will never dare oppose, but follow you in terror."

" Choose me," said the eagle. " I am lord of the upper air. Choose me and you will have power to leave the earth and fly on the very back of the wind. I will take you to borders of the sky; there, from heights unknown to man, you shall see everything that happens below. When you enter Jerusalem

THE DONKEY OF GOD

flying between my strong wings, the people will believe you are a god and they will worship."

" Choose me," said the mole. " I go where the eagle is helpless and the lion cannot follow. Choose me and I will give you the keys of earth. I will guide you to the roots of power, to secrets buried beneath the stones. I know where every vein of gold is hidden ; my home is among caves of rubies, hills of emerald, ledges of pure diamond. Choose me and you will be greater than the greatest ; you will be able to buy empires ; you will not only be a king, but King of kings."

" The great ones laugh at treasures," whispered the fox. " Who but a fool desires gold and glittering pebbles that turn men against each other with greed and jealousy. Choose me and I will give you cunning. I will show you how to outwit all men and overcome your enemies with shrewdness. Choose me and I will teach you cleverness that is better than wealth and craft that is stronger than strength."

" Craft ! " trumpeted the elephant. " Craft and cunning are for knaves who will never be wise. Choose me and I will give you true wisdom. I am the oldest of living creatures ; my years span a century and I have watched the comings and goings of all the races. Choose me and you will rule the changing mind of the unchanging world."

" Choose me," lowed the cow. " I am sacred. India and Egypt worship me. I feed the world."

THE DONKEY OF GOD

"Choose me," bellowed the dragon. "I will spread fire before you and magic wherever you go."

"Choose me!" neighed the horse. "I am swift as rage. The glory of my nostrils is terrible to the enemy. I swallow the ground; I laugh at fear."

"Choose me!" screamed the camel. "Choose me! Choose me!" cried all the animals separately and in chorus. Only the donkey was silent.

"And what can you give?" asked Jesus, speaking for the first time and turning to the dusty little fellow. "What have you to promise?"

"Nothing," murmured the donkey. "Nothing. I am the lowest of all God's creatures and the least."

But Jesus remembered. "The lowest shall be lifted up," he said, "and the last shall be first."

And so the meekest of men chose the meekest of animals. And they entered Jerusalem together.

But the great moment passed. Proud Jerusalem sneered at the carpenter's son even as it had stoned the prophets before him, and only a handful of poor folk listened to his words. He was despised and rejected. The people turned against him. He was imprisoned on a false charge and condemned to death. They put a crown of thorns upon his head, mocked him and made him carry his own cross.

THE DONKEY OF GOD

It was while Jesus was struggling up the hill that the donkey saw him for the last time. Their sad eyes met.

" No," said Jesus. " You cannot help me now. Yet, since you have done more for me than have most men, you shall be rewarded. I cannot undo what God has done; what He has ordained must be carried out. But I can soften His decree. True, you will have to fetch and carry and feed on thorns. Yet these things will never again be hard for you. Because you carried me three times, so shall you be able to carry three times as much as animals thrice your size—and your load will seem lighter than theirs. You suffered thorns for my sake; so shall you be nourished when others can find nothing to feed on. You shall eat the thorns and nettles of the field— and they shall taste like sweet salads. You bore me when I grew to manhood, when I was a child, and even my mother before I was born. So shall you bear my cross—but you shall bear it without pain. Here—! " And as Jesus touched the shoulders of the donkey, a velvet-black cross appeared on the back of the kneeling animal.

And Jesus, shouldering his burden, climbed up Calvary . . .

THE DONKEY OF GOD

Francis heard the last syllable leave his lips in a kind of wonder. His tiredness had gone: everything in him was full of strength. He was surprised to see that the sun had set and that a little horned moon had come into the sky, one horn pointing to Assisi. He thought he understood the sign. When he turned back, the donkey had disappeared. The field was dark. But a light greater than the moon's was on Francis' face.

THE HILL-TOWNS—2

GUBBIO—SAN GIMIGNANO—SIENA

SAN GIMIGNANO

GUBBIO—SAN GIMIGNANO—SIENA

DON'T, I warn you, mistake the story of " The Donkey of God " for Scripture. The part about the Creation is, of course, in the Bible, although told somewhat differently, and the incident about Jesus and the clay pigeons that flew away is a legend many hundreds of years old. The rest is true only in spirit. And it is true, I hope, to the spirit of Saint Francis.

The story of Francis does not end with his vision of the donkey; it was, I like to believe, the beginning of his holy career. Anyone can see that, as far as the donkey is concerned, everything that was predicted for him has come true. He eats thorny twigs and stinging nettles as though they were smooth grasses. He carries loads that would break the back of an animal three times his size. And if you are ever in Sardinia you will see that the native donkey has on his grey back two black lines that form a perfect cross.

So much for the donkey. The rest of Francis' story is now history. He returned to Assisi, gave up the reckless associa-

THE DONKEY OF GOD

tions of his past, and, devoting himself to the poor, began a new life. His reputation for goodness and simplicity spread throughout Europe. Others soon came to believe as he did; followers gathered about him. He founded the now famous Order of the Franciscans seven hundred years ago. Immediately after his death in 1226, legends sprang up about his life and works.

Eighty years later the painter Giotto, coming to Assisi, used many of the incidents that were said to have happened. Now, though the colours are beginning to fade, Giotto's paintings in the great church in Assisi show Saint Francis renouncing the world, expelling evil spirits from the town of Arezzo, curing the wounded, saving a child who had fallen from a tower, appearing in a vision, ascending to Heaven in Elijah's chariot of fire. And, although he is not shown talking to the donkey, you can see him in the loveliest and most famous of these frescoes—preaching to the birds. The expression of the Saint is a study in contrasts. His back is bent in humility, his brow is calm; but his hands are lifted in argument, evidently proving some difficult point. As for the birds, they cluster about the Saint like a small but faithful congregation. Their attitude is faultless: their heads are slightly bowed and their eyes are on the preacher rather than on each other. They hover in the air, literally hanging on his words. I have seen many a more notable congregation less patient.

GUBBIO—SAN GIMIGNANO—SIENA

Gubbio, although some distance from Assisi, is still in the Saint Francis country. One of its favourite legends—the legend of the Wolf of Gubbio—has been made into countless stories, parables and playlets; there is even a full-length rhymed drama (" The Wolf of Gubbio ") by Josephine Preston Peabody. Some say the wolf was an actual beast, the wildest one in the province of Umbria, and that his robberies and killings were ruining the countryside. Homes were despoiled, children devoured, villages terrorised. Francis resolved to stop it. Friends warned him against the rash attempt; soldiers who had failed said that it was not a wolf at all but a werewolf, a devilish spirit sent by Satan.

" All the more reason why the creature must be talked to," said Francis.

" Talked to ! " exclaimed his friends. " Exterminated, you mean. And surely you don't intend to go to Gubbio without weapons ! Reason with him if you will, but reason with a sword ! "

But Francis remembered how the poet Horace had gone into just such a wood armed with nothing but a clear conscience. " Horace did not flinch when he saw a wolf because

THE DONKEY OF GOD

he was more protected by goodness than by shields or javelins," said Francis, " and Horace was a heathen. What, then, have I to fear who have the added protection of the cross ? "

So, though his advisers shook their heads, Francis journeyed through bush and brake toward where the wolf had last been seen. He did not have far to go. Soon a shaggy monster, the very counterpart of Horace's Sabine terror, fierce as a lion " with a head like death's," stood snarling in the path. Francis clutched his cross. But, after a moment, he dropped it from his hand.

" It is hardly fair," he thought, " to use so great a power against one misguided animal. Even if this is the fiend himself I must be fair with him." So, just as the creature was about to spring, Francis said, " Let us talk this over, Brother Wolf."

The wolf paused. He looked before he leaped. This was something strange. Anger he knew ; curses and cries of fear were all part of the day's work ; spears and arrows made him all the fiercer. But kind words were unknown to him, and a calm face promised a new experience. The wolf stopped snarling ; he would see what sort of human this was before he devoured him.

And so Francis reasoned with the curious beast. He told the wolf that all living things were related since all were members of God's family. He told how God had given all of his

GUBBIO—SAN GIMIGNANO—SIENA

children special gifts—fleetness to the deer, quills to the porcupine, a house of horn to the snail, wings to the bird, hoofs to the horse, a solid fort to the turtle, sword-like tusks to the elephant, and strength to the wolf. But, continued Francis, only a coward abuses his gifts, only a coward uses his strength to frighten the weak—and the wolf, surely, was no coward. And Francis went on to tell about all the good things that wolves had done, beginning with the wolf who mothered the homeless twins, Romulus and Remus, and had helped found the greatest of cities. And he spoke not only of what wolves had accomplished, but of the great things that a wolf might do.

Five hours later, when Francis' friends searched the wood, they found the Saint slumbering on a stone. And at his side, as though guarding the sleeper, sat the wolf, his head resting on the Saint's knees. And never again, so ends the tale, was a single hen stolen from the coops of the town; not a child was molested, not a babe frightened. On the contrary, the wolf became the guardian of Gubbio. He walked its streets like an honoured citizen, and when he died his portrait was painted on the walls of Gubbio's proud Palace of the Consuls.

That is one version. Other story-tellers give a more realistic account. The wolf, according to them, was not a wolf at all, but a robber-chieftain who was so savage that he had been nick-named " The Wolf of Gubbio." He had been one of Francis' gay companions in his younger days, but had grown

THE DONKEY OF GOD

wild and bitter, hating all men and sparing none. On one of its raiding expeditions, his band captured Francis (it is also thought that Francis set out to get captured) and brought him before their leader. No one knows what happened between the two; no one can say whether Francis was recognised, whether he was saved by memory or a miracle. But the tale goes that nothing more was heard of the marauders. The band disappeared; Gubbio was at peace; the farmers lost no more children, chickens or sleep. And the stoutest of Francis' new disciples, according to this legend, was a tall, black-browed monk whom Francis affectionately called " Brother Wolf."

But Gubbio consists of more than legends. Its position on the slope of a mighty mountain, its high fortifications, its protected roads winding among the hills to Perugia point to its importance in the Middle Ages. Furthermore, Gubbio is one of the few towns which have kept a distinctly medieval character. The Fifteenth Century is still at home here; except for American sewing-machines and a battered car or two, the Nineteen Hundreds have never entered these twisted, time-coloured streets. When you stand on the balcony of the Palace of the Consuls (one of the most impressive Gothic halls in Italy) and view the peaks and valleys that stretch beneath, you are no longer looking at the everyday world, but at a brighter if more brutal world that lives only in the imagination—or in Gubbio.

GUBBIO—SAN GIMIGNANO—SIENA

Yet, in spite of all its glamorous associations, I remember Gubbio not only because of its history or its fantasy. I remember it as the place where I first ate finocchio. Let me say at once that finocchio is not a delicacy nor some rare sweetmeat; finocchio is only a vegetable. But what a vegetable! Fennel is the English name—it can even be found in the lanes of Cornwall or, four thousand miles away, in the sub-tropical Bermudas. But the wild fennel is nothing but a poor and rude relation of the well-established and carefully brought up finocchio. The true finocchio is something like a round-hearted, tenderer celery with an aromatic licorice flavour. To some the combination is as bad as a combination of chocolate and onions —two excellent flavours but scarcely improved when mixed; to others it is a heavenly blend. I confess to being one of those who find the mixture of celery and anise delicious, especially when served as a salad. There are two favourite ways of enjoying this dish: uncooked and dipped in salt, or baked in olive oil and powdered with finely grated cheese. Either way should give you strength as well as pleasure for, if you can believe the Italians, it is one of the most health-producing of plants. There is, in fact, a legend that illustrates how highly its powers are regarded; and, since it relates not only to finocchio but to Francis, I shall repeat it.

Shortly after Francis had tamed the Wolf of Gubbio, he was called to help the people of another city. The way was long

THE DONKEY OF GOD

and the crossroads confusing. Two of his fellow-monks made the journey with him and, on the third day, it was discovered that they had little food and nothing to drink. Worse was to follow. While trudging over a mountain, the pack which held their remaining provisions fell and was lost in the ravine below. Nevertheless, Francis continued with the pilgrimage, regardless of the lack of supplies. After three more days the sufferings of his companions were unbearable and the two monks began to reproach their leader. He bore their complaints without replying. The heat was intense, the glare terrific. But Francis uncovered his head and knelt down.

"Mother Earth and Brother Sun," he prayed, "the most unworthy of your family implores you. Not for himself, but for his two companions who need to be nourished more than he."

When he rose, his companions cried, "A miracle!" For where Francis had knelt, a spring of sweet water was bubbling. And at the border of the spring were three bulbs of the whitest finocchio. Refreshed with these, the brethren continued their journey, gathering strength with every mile. Finally when the distant town was reached, the travellers were less fatigued than when they started.

And ever since then, so the story-tellers end as they smack their lips, the vigorous white hearts of finocchio are given a place of honour on the tables of the mighty as well as those of the humble.

GUBBIO—SAN GIMIGNANO—SIENA

Enough has been said about the antique spirit that still finds its home in the hill-towns; and by the time you come to San Gimignano you will have exhausted your whole supply of adjectives. Keep one or two, I advise; for if you want to see how a hill-town looked six hundred years ago, and you must choose only one town, let it be San Gimignano. San Gimignano is to Italy what Carcassonne is to France and Old Nuremberg is to Germany. The mediaeval town walls still surround the heights; three of the early gates maintain their vigilance; the gaunt piazza makes the occasional motor-car ashamed of its youth. The streets are so absorbed in their ancient windings and unwindings that they would scarcely be surprised to see Dante walk through them as he did in the year 1300 when he came here as an envoy from Florence.

But it is the panorama of mounting stones which has given San Gimignano the title of " The City of Beautiful Towers." They are curious structures. At first glimpse they look modern—as you approach, the town takes on the sky-line of an American city in miniature—and it is hard to believe that the twin towers of the Ardinghelli (one of the " first families "

THE DONKEY OF GOD

of San Gimignano, always on the look-out for attacks) were erected in the Thirteenth Century.

The cathedral is even older—two hundred years older, say the authorities—and it boasts a particularly fine set of frescoes, illustrating the story of Santa Fina, by the artist Ghirlandaio. Nor should you leave the town without visiting the Church of Saint Augustine, if only to see the gem-like murals depicting that saint's career by Benozzo Gozzoli, of whom you will hear more when you come to Florence.

But there are hills to climb and legends to learn before we reach Florence, "the pride of Tuscany." Anticipating Florence, we must become acquainted with her age-long rival, "serene and splendid Siena."

Citizens of Siena still talk as if their city were separated not only from its neighbours, but from the rest of Italy. And this is not so strange, as Siena has always prided itself on its independence—independence in government, in character, and (as early as the Thirteenth Century) in art. Considered as an art-centre, Siena is a museum of museums, a priceless treasure-house where one amazement leads to another. Here, crowning the three hills on which the town is built, is the Piazza del Campo, the great square where the races are run— of which there will be more later—and the richly decorated Palazzo Publico with its slender tower, the lordliest in Italy, a combination of observatory, fortified spire, bell-tower and

GUBBIO—SAN GIMIGNANO—SIENA

obelisk. Here is the Academy of Fine Arts with its comprehensive showing of native artists. Here, in Lorenzetti's frescoes in the town hall or on the painted *tavolette* (tablets or covers) of the tax-reports—a series of masterpieces in miniature—you can trace the history of Siena from the earliest days to the Sixteenth Century. Here is the house where Saint Catherine of Siena was born and lived most of her life—the rooms of the house having been made into small but splendid chapels—and here is the Church of San Domenico where Catherine had her visions and where her ecstasy has been painted around the altar which is her shrine.

And here, outshining its rivals, is the stupendous cathedral,

THE DONKEY OF GOD

built entirely of glittering marble, which stands on the highest piece of ground, on the foundations of what was once a temple to Minerva. It is not a mere building, it is a series of climaxes carved in stone. The facade of many-coloured marble is one of the noblest of Pisano's noble designs; inside, the zebra-like columns, made of stripes of black and white, are intensified by the terra-cotta busts above the great arches. The pavement is gay with designs half-drawn, half-inlaid in the marble; the host of figures on Pisano's pulpit—one of the richest in the world—can be studied for hours; the great Piccolomini altar has four statues by Michelangelo.

Yet, admitting all these wonders, the thing I remember most of Siena's indoors is one small room of the cathedral—the library. It was built in 1495 by order of the Cardinal Piccolomini (who became Pope Pius III) to house the books left to him by his uncle who had been Pope Pius II. When you enter this chamber it is as if you had stepped into the centre of a flashing jewel. This effect is due to the brilliant mural paintings by Pinturicchio, a set showing incidents in the life of Aeneas Piccolomini (Pius II), which cover practically every inch of the wall. The room vibrates with colour, colour in action. The walls extend themselves; the entire room expands into vast fields, crowded courts, toppling towns. By a miracle of drawing, a few feet of canvas lead down the long aisles of Saint Peter's in Rome or over the heights of Ancona and out

GUBBIO—SAN GIMIGNANO—SIENA

to a sea that loses itself in an unfathomed sky. Here, pulsing with more life than life itself, is a panorama of the Fifteenth Century, more vivid than all the books ever written about it.

Yet nothing within four walls is as glorious as Siena itself—its hilly streets, its atmosphere, its very being. The spirit of Siena cannot be contained in the most sumptuous structure built by man; it cannot be housed even in " the house of God." It may be found in the most inconspicuous places, in the shabbiest alleys as surely as in the great piazza or central square.

It is in the by-ways that you will hear most about the *palio*—that characteristic horse-race whose origin is lost in the Dark Ages. Although the *palio*, in one form or another, has been run for about a thousand years, it is as keenly contested to-day as ever. Even in modern Siena—if you call Siena modern at all—the race is the year's principal event; fierce blows are exchanged on the course; the crowds are just as feverish as when armour was ordinary iron clothing instead of museum-pieces. It is the story of a certain *palio*—one that happened in about 1500—that is told in the following tale, " The Horse of Siena."

THE HORSE OF SIENA

THERE WERE WINGS, UNEARTHLY WINGS, IN THE PLAZA TO-DAY

THE HORSE OF SIENA

PEPPI and his brother Fabio lived in a side-street of the Valle Piatta, almost the narrowest and certainly the darkest alley in old Siena. The room they shared was a poor cellar in the poorest district in a city that had once been the proudest of hill-towns. It still was one of the fairest; and, though endless wars with Florence, its oldest enemy, had drained its money-chests, Siena was still " the bright pearl in the crown of Tuscany." At least so its poets claimed—and there were plenty of poets to supply verses for every occasion, for great events and small ones, for funerals and holiday-wishes, for weddings and business cards, and especially for the winning of the great race known as the palio.

Every *contrada* or ward had its own poet—there were seventeen of them in Peppi's time—and the poets hated each other as heartily as the ward they represented despised every other ward. Each *contrada* had its distinctive emblem, its separate name, its different colours. And you can be sure that each district was certain its own colours made the finest show and its citizens were the noblest, while the banners of the other sixteen districts were dirty rags that floated over an evil lot of purse-snatchers, candle-robbers, cut-throats, and assorted criminals.

Peppi believed all this. The only three people he knew—his brother Fabio, Bennuccio the baker and Piero the poet—had told him so. When the time for the running of the palio drew near, Bennuccio grew bitterer day by day.

" Wait till you're a little older," said the baker as the boy sat on a flour-cask and gnawed a heel of bread. " You'll see what I tell you is true."

And he launched out on the tale which Peppi enjoyed as much with each rehearsal as though he heard it for the first time.

" Once the Snail was the most prosperous ward of all the seventeen and they used to say that one Snail was worth two Dragons, three Eagles and a riverful of Tortoises. That angered them all, especially the Tortoises who—worse luck!—had the ward next to ours. They became our worst rivals and continually schemed to ruin us. They knew they could never get the upper hand in fair fight—we defeated them in every race and outsung them in all the song-contests. So they tried bribery, mud-throwing, even kidnapping our patron saint from his chapel. But it did them no good. It was our own patriotism that ruined us. When Florence sent her third army against us twelve years ago—the year you were born, Peppi—the men of the Snail ward rushed to arms. Your father was one of the first to go—and he never came back. But the Tortoises had been waiting for just such a chance. Only a few of them took up arms against the attackers—only enough to make a showing—the rest claimed there was a fever in the ward and they could not leave their beds. When the great battle was finally won and the Florentines were driven back, less than half of our men came home. The cowardly Tortoises, who now outnumbered us three to one, claimed their share of the spoils. There were weeks of rioting, but when the traitors brought in hired Eagles to help them, we were defeated. They took not only their share of the spoils, to which they had no right, but our share as well. To this day every Snail knows the Tortoise people are as filthy as they are false. It is said they live on poisons that would kill any honest man, and we have a proverb, 'Catch a Tortoise and you'll find a snake.' Don't forget that, Peppi."

"I won't," the boy would answer solemnly as Bennuccio would finish, and he meant it. Then back he would go to the cellar where he kept house for his brother Fabio. Fabio was restless, bold-eyed, quick-tongued, light for his age. His dapper build and pocket-size made him the ideal jockey; and though he had won no races for his ward as yet, he was always assuring his supporters he would be the hero of the next palio.

THE DONKEY OF GOD

" I've only had three chances," he would say to his friends at the wine-shop, " and all were on packs of bones fit for the tanner's yard. I could have ridden faster on a broom ! Wait until the Snail draws a decent horse for the palio, and all the other ward-jockeys will see of me will be my dust in their eyes ! "

Being a jockey, Fabio, naturally, had to take good care of himself. He had to eat well, drink as often as friends would invite him, sleep late and not waste any of his strength. Above all—now that he was in training to win the prize for his ward—he could not permit himself any hard work. Of course, some one had to take care of the room, cook the meals, find the food somehow and bring Fabio back from the tavern on nights when Fabio was not feeling well. And since there was no one else to do it except Peppi, Peppi did it. Peppi had no time to sleep late for there was much to do in the mornings if he wanted to earn enough pennies for meals. Nor could Peppi eat well—in fact, he was glad that he could eat at all. But then, eating wasn't important as far as he was concerned. Peppi was not going to reflect honour on his ward ; he was not going to do anything except carry bread for Bennuccio the baker ; he was lucky to have a place to live in and luckier to have a brother as wonderful as Fabio.

Peppi regarded his brother with the adoration one gives saints and heroes, and Fabio accepted it as his due. Peppi was

THE HORSE OF SIENA

twelve years old and undersized; no one except Bennuccio and Piero had ever looked at him twice. Fabio was eighteen, smart, straight-limbed; and when the young jockey wore his red cap, girls turned to smile at him. If the jockey-god in the story (the god who rode the horses of the sun) had come down from heaven to live in Siena, Peppi could not have laboured for him any harder or more happily than he worked for his brother. Money was scarce, food was hard to get; but Peppi was proud to serve such a hero as Fabio. " Besides," he always ended to Bennuccio, as he crammed a crust in his pocket, " something is sure to make things easier."

Something did. One evening Fabio came home earlier than usual. Peppi could see he was excited, and there was a new scarlet cap with yellow braid on his head.

" We're in luck! " cried Fabio. " The Council met to-day, and one of the horses for the next palio is going to be stabled in the alley next to ours. And we're going to take care of it."

" We? " asked Peppi innocently.

" Yes, we," answered Fabio. " Of course you will do the simple, ordinary work—preparing his mash and carrying his food and curry-combing him and sweeping his stall and washing the saddle and bringing him fresh hay twice a week and —oh, just keeping him healthy. I will do the harder work— the sort of thing that needs experience—looking him over and seeing if he's in condition."

THE DONKEY OF GOD

" But how did the Council know about us—I mean how did they know—? " Here Peppi paused uncomfortably.

" Oh," said Fabio, airily, " I suppose every one in Siena has heard how I would have won the race last year if my horse had been better groomed and if that fool horse-shoer had shod him properly and if the other jockeys hadn't conspired together to crowd me off the track and if I hadn't felt a little dizzy at the beginning. As it was, I came in seventh out of ten, didn't I ? "

" You did, Fabio," Peppi answered him. " And you would have been first if it hadn't been for your enemies who won the saint's favour away. You forget that."

" True," said Fabio. " I must remember that, too. Well, at least the Council had heard of me. And, oh—now that I think of it—it seems your friend Bennuccio had put in a word for you—I mean for us. So don't worry your head about it any longer, but trot out the supper. I've been waiting all afternoon at the plaza to get the news, and I'm simply starving. You don't know what it is to stand around from noon till suppertime with nothing but a glass or two and half a cake in all that time."

Peppi did not. During the next six months standing around became even less possible. Added to his regular work and the hundred odd jobs to be performed for Fabio, there was the horse to be looked after.

THE HORSE OF SIENA

At first Peppi detested the animal. He was an ill-favoured brute, to begin with. Besides, he was spavined and knock-kneed; his hooves interfered with each other; his head had a way of jerking back as if he were about to throw something off his shoulders, and he had a wild look in his eye. " An evil eye," said Fabio and would have nothing more to do with him.

But after two weeks Peppi realised that the wild look was the look of hunger, and it did not take the boy long to decide that the poor beast had never had enough to eat in all his life. It was also plain that he never would get enough, no matter how long he might live. The Council's allowance bought just enough grain to take the edge off the horse's appetite and Peppi was soon dividing his own bread with him and begging Bennuccio for the ends of stale loaves.

" You'll spoil that handsome steed of yours," the baker would laugh. " If you keep on pampering him, he'll refuse to recognise the humble citizens of the Snail ward and talk only to horses that draw the royal coach. But if any one can make anything out of that collection of misfit ribs, you're the boy—so take what you need." And he would slip an extra bun in, saying, " That's for you, Peppi, not for your bony baby —nor for your brother, either. Fabio's getting a little fat and we don't want the light of the ward to get too heavy, do we ? "

Peppi found it hard to tell when Bennuccio was joking and when he was serious. He was joking, of course, when he named

THE DONKEY OF GOD

the horse. " Did you ever see such wooden supports ! " he had cried. " Regular peg-legs." And the name had stuck. Peg-leg he became, even to Peppi. But as the months went by and Peppi tended the old nag more and more, he grew fond of the despised stallion and shortened the mocking name to Peg.

" And a good name, too," said Piero the poet, with a smile that went up at one corner. " Especially for a white horse—I presume he *is* white, or would be if it weren't for his grey hairs."

" Yes," said Peppi cautiously. " I *think* he's white. But Peg is short for Peg-leg."

" And for Pegasus," smiled the poet.

" Peg-as-us ? " inquired Peppi, stumbling over the strange syllables. " What sort of horse was he ? "

" He was what every horse would like to be," answered Piero. " Can you imagine a horse with hooves of silver, a mane soft and thick as a waving cloud, a neck strong as a Roman arch and ' clothed in thunder,' a broad back smooth as lake-water, and an eye of pure fire ? Well, if you've imagined all this—and it's more than most people could do—you would still have no idea of how Pegasus looked. For in addition to all these perfections there was a greater one. From the shoulder-blades of Pegasus there sprouted two of the widest, whitest, most powerful wings that ever fanned the skies. They shone like soft lightning, even in the dark, and great legends and

THE HORSE OF SIENA

splendid poems were written by those lucky enough to find one of the quill-feathers. Only the archangel Michael wore a grander pair, and even his, though rainbow-coloured, were no swifter than those of Pegasus. Have you ever seen a humming-bird above a flower, balancing on nothing but air, its wings going so fast that all you can see is the tiny body darting like a living emerald? Magnify that a thousand times, change the quick green to alabaster-white and you'll have Pegasus—except that Pegasus was as much faster than a humming-bird as a humming-bird is faster than a—" the poet thought a moment and then spat out the word—" a tortoise. You can believe that such a creature would not stand to any one's hitching-post. Only the gods could put a halter on him; only the heroes and poets could ride him—and even they could not always keep their seats. Although he came down to earth at certain rare times, his favourite pastures were the sky and it was no uncommon thing for Pegasus to bound from a river-valley to the highest mountain peak and then, with a sudden beat of those mighty wings, to scale the walls of heaven."

Peppi held his breath. This was a horse, indeed. A horse for heroes—and (hadn't Piero said it?) for poets. Then he said shyly, " Piero, have you ever ridden—him ? "

Piero smiled and frowned at the same time.

" Sometimes I think I have," answered the Snails' poet. " At other times—" He shrugged. " Once or twice I've been

THE DONKEY OF GOD

fairly sure I've—well, if not ridden, at least mounted him. But it must have been in a dream."

" But you've seen him, haven't you ? " insisted Peppi.

" Also in dreams. He isn't to be seen every day or by every eye, I can promise you."

" But he isn't dead, is he ? " asked Peppi.

" By no means," answered Piero promptly. " No ; he's living, and as noble-spirited and heaven-searching—or sky-larking—as ever. But he's grown shyer. He was at home with the old gods and the older races. When men stopped believing in the gods who were his playmates, they stopped believing in him, too. That hurt his pride. He scarcely ever visits earth now—and when he does it's almost always in disguise. But, though I can't be sure of having seen his foot-prints, I can swear that I have heard the music of his wings. And I never cease to pray to him. As one lover of horses to another, Peppi, you might do the same."

" I will ! I will ! " cried the boy eagerly. And he added Pegasus to his favourite saints along with Saint Bernardino and Saint John and Saint Augustine and the beloved Saint Catherine of Siena.

The months crawled around. The almond boughs shook off the snow ; unfolded their blossoms ; then snowed again. The ancient olive-trees twisted themselves into newer and stranger shapes. The cruel cactus softened and set out clusters of

THE HORSE OF SIENA

sweet figs among its bitter thorns. Grapes rounded, reddened, ripened. . . . But Peppi never forgot. He tended the earthly Peg with his hands and prayed to the heavenly Pegasus in his heart. Even with all Peppi's devotion, Peg never lost his boniness nor his awkward, stumbling gait. But to his keeper's loving eye, the old nag's coat seemed smoother and, if his legs were not as straight as they might have been, at least they kept his body up. Besides, Peppi comforted himself, the other horses were not much better.

Spring and summer dragged on. Then, before he was aware of it, it was August—August, the month of the great race. All was excitement now. Every ward was a hive of gossip, last-minute plans, secret treaties and even more secret treacheries. Then on the thirteenth—unlucky day for most!—the Council met, the wooden boards which protected the race-course were taken up, and the plaza was made ready for the first trials. Cartloads of sand were emptied on the glistening roadway; wooden platforms blocked up the shop-windows; the colours of the rival wards began to show themselves.

But this, Peppi knew, was nothing compared to what would happen in three days. This was only the tuning-up of the players, the trumpets and challenges before the battle itself. And yet everything depended on what happened in the next few hours—for there were seventeen horses ready for the trials and only ten would be chosen to run. And no one—

not even the Council itself—knew what the choice would be.

The morning of August thirteenth was a bright promise. Seven o'clock. No one was within doors; every one was out in the streets—even bed-ridden invalids were up, dragging chairs with them. Eight o'clock. The churches in seventeen wards were crowded; the statues of seventeen patron saints listened to the prayers of seven times seventeen priests. Eight thirty. Seventeen horses of every age, kind and colour were being led, pushed, coaxed, commanded, and jostled toward the plaza in the centre of Siena. Nine o'clock. And the plaza was packed to its last inch—Bennuccio said even the stone walls stretched to let the crowds in—as the Council mounted its stand.

In front of the three Councillors was a small table which every one could see. On the table were two bowls of clear glass with seventeen pieces of paper in each bowl. Seventeen numbers, corresponding to the horses, lay in one bowl; the names of the seventeen wards lay in the other. A bell spoke suddenly from the top of a tower and one of the Council rose and held up his hand. There was one last loud buzz of talk, then a breathing silence as the Councillor in scarlet stirred the papers in both bowls with a small whip tipped with silver. Then the Councillor in purple stood up and, putting one hand in each bowl, held up two slips of paper for the third Councillor to read. This official, clad in crimson, called out " Number Five ! "

THE HORSE OF SIENA

Number Five was a large roan-coloured mare, not handsome, but strongly built, and the crowd seemed to hang upon the announcer until he called the name of the ward. " Number Five," he repeated, " will represent the Dragon."

What a roar went up then, especially from the ward whose rowdy citizens were referred to as fire-eaters ! Cheers and cat-calls tore the air, and the trumpets had to speak twice before the crowds grew silent and the next pair of selections could be made.

Again the papers in the bowl were mixed by the first Councillor, two slips taken out by the second, and the announcement made by the third.

" Number Three—is awarded to the Eagle."

" What an ill-favoured beast," muttered the Captain of the Giraffe, who would have praised the horse as a beauty if it had been awarded to the Giraffe. A moment later the announcer called :

" Number Six—to the Giraffe ! "

And though Number Six was a thick-barrelled dray-horse, " Now *that's* a powerful fellow ! " cried the Captain of the Giraffe, while his henchmen shouted themselves out of breath.

So the balloting went on with shrieks and shameless jokes, cries of approval and curses of despair. Peppi, held high on Bennuccio's shoulder, heard them all.

THE DONKEY OF GOD

" Number One—the Unicorn ! "

" Number Eight—the Owl ! "

So far none of the high numbers had been chosen—and his Peg was Number Seventeen ! Then Peppi heard the announcer call " Sixteen "—and Peppi could feel the crowd draw tight as a stretched wire, for Number Sixteen, a knotty little bay, had won last year's palio. His heart skipped a beat as he heard the Councillor completing his sentence "—to the Tortoise."

" May Saint Bernardino send the plague on 'em ! " swore Bennuccio. " Are those traitorous Tortoises to have everything their own way ! I smell filthy work here. That Councillor knew the look of those papers. Bribery again, my boy."

But Peppi said nothing. He was waiting, waiting with clenched hands and an iron band tightening around his chest.

" Number Nine—the Goose."

" Number Thirteen—the Porcupine."

Peppi had been keeping count on stiff fingers. Eight had been selected. Two more names and the first ten would have been chosen.

" Number Eleven—the She-Wolf."

The greatest roar went up now. Number Eleven was a pop-

THE HORSE OF SIENA

ular animal and the she-wolf was the sacred emblem of all Siena. The little candle of hope that had been burning inside of Peppi went out. One more—and it was all over. The people on the outer edges of the crowd were beginning to drift back to their wards. Then Pippi heard the third Councillor call, as if from a great distance.

" Seventeen—"

Seventeen ! Why, that was Peg ! His own Peg would have a chance to run. That, at least, was something. Then—and he could not believe he had really heard it—the announcer finished his last sentence.

" —to the Snail."

It was true, then ! Bennuccio's roar of delight told him so. It was a miracle, nothing less. His own horse to represent his own ward—and to be ridden by his own brother ! Of course it was a miracle ! What did it matter that the Tortoises were jeering, " Snails for the Snail—that's what their four-legged insect looks like ! " What if others were jeering with them. Peppi's heart had leaped like Pegasus with one bound from a bottomless pit and was soaring from sky to sky. He could even feel the wings beat in his breast. He kissed fat Bennuccio; he hugged Piero the poet; he wanted to throw his arms around every one, including the Councillors and all seventeen saints. That night Peppi went to sleep the happiest soul in Siena.

THE DONKEY OF GOD

Twelve hours later he was the most miserable boy in all Italy. Fabio had left the house early in the morning. About noon he had returned, with a flushed face, saying the horse wasn't fit to ride on.

"Not fit to ride on?" Peppi had faltered. "But Peg's better than he's been in months."

"Well, I don't like his looks!" Fabio had muttered, with shame-faced anger. "He offered to bite me when I was in his stall this morning. And he's got a queer red in his eye. Let some one else ride him. I won't!" And he had left without eating his lunch—a most unusual thing for Fabio.

Then Fabio disappeared. Supper-time came; evening followed; lamps were lighted. But Fabio did not return. That night Peppi did not sleep. He waited, lighting one candle-end after another; now heating a little rice; now running to the end of the alley and trying to see beyond the dark street. He was feverish but awake when the grey dawn crept into the room and then the loud day. But still no Fabio. What to do? Where to go?... Hardly knowing how he got there, Peppi found himself at Bennuccio's.

"Yes, my lad, I've heard," the baker told him. "And I've heard some things I'd rather not hear."

"Is there anything wrong with Fabio?" was Peppi's first question.

"Wrong with Fabio?" Bennuccio wrinkled his brows.

THE HORSE OF SIENA

" Well, since you put it that way—yes and no. But don't you worry about your precious brother. You sit down just where you are and drink this cup of coffee. Oh, it isn't strong enough to hurt—just strong enough to hold you up. You need it, my boy. You look like the ghost of a ghost." He went to the front of his shop. " Ha ! Here's Piero coming. Now you nibble this cinnamon-bun like the mouse you are while Piero tells us the news."

It didn't look like the same Piero to Peppi. Instead of the playful, flashing-eyed poet, here was a gloomy and black-browed man. But everything looked wrong to Peppi this morning.

" Well ? " asked Bennuccio.

" You were right," said Piero, biting off his sentences. " The swine ! Forty silver crowns. The Tortoises can afford it. He jumped at the chance. Some stuff to make him easily sick. Fool the doctor. I'd like to wring his neck ! "

What money ? Who jumped at what chance ? Whose neck did Piero want to wring ? The doctor's ? Whatever could they be talking about ?

" But Fabio ? " cried Peppi. " Bennuccio said you'd have news about Fabio ! "

" I told you not to worry," said the baker, with a gruff gentleness. " There's nothing wrong with your brother—nothing wrong with his body at any rate. Is there, Piero ? "

THE DONKEY OF GOD

"Not yet," answered the poet, grimly. "Not yet."

Peppi could not understand it. Still, Fabio was safe, and that was something. Perhaps he would be home this afternoon—perhaps he was there now.

"I've got to—look after Peg," said Peppi, and got to his feet.

"And don't forget your prayers," reminded Piero. "If ever the Snails needed divine help, they will need it to-morrow."

To-morrow! As if Peppi could forget it! The word was like a mountain on his heart. The sun was flooding the city when Peppi left the baker's, but he groped down the alley as if he were feeling his way through mist. Blindly, he opened the door of Peg's stable, let his feet guide him along the rough boards, and found himself in the dingy stall.

Gradually his eyes grew accustomed to the darkness. Now he could see the broken plaster-cast of Saint Catherine—Cecco the sacristan had given it to him—now the greyish-white flanks of the horse, now his head. Peppi put his arm around the ungraceful neck and began to weep. It seemed to him that the animal understood, for he nuzzled the boy's shoulder and whinnied softly. It was as if he were trying to say something. Poor Peg! If he only knew! But maybe he did, thought Peppi. Maybe he could even help. But what could an animal do? It was divine help, Piero said, that was needed. He would pray—here. And now. He began, "Our Father . . ." In the

THE HORSE OF SIENA

midst of the prayer his tired head sank and his eyes closed.

Now it seemed to Peppi that a light had come into the stable—a light he could *hear*—and his forehead felt as if a great wind swept over it. When he opened his eyes the stable had grown into a cave whose ends he could not see, but all was made of crystal. Rounded walls and sky-like ceiling were soft with a blue radiance; the floor was marble to the eyes but velvet to the touch. In the very centre of the cave stood Saint Catherine, and her arm was about the neck of Peg—a shining, straight-legged Peg with a mane soft and thick as combed wool, hooves of silver, eyes of fire and a neck like a Roman arch. Two wings shone from the shoulder-blades, wings in which the feathers were quivering as if they had just stopped beating the air. As the hooves pawed the ground, Peppi heard a muffled thunder and knew he was looking at Pegasus.

Then it seemed as if the crystal in the cave rang softly; the ringing turned into a word; and the word was the word of Saint Catherine.

"Do not despair," sang the Saint in a voice like fountains at play. "Your prayers have been heard—and they will be answered. To-morrow I will be with you."

"And I will be with you, too," said Pegasus—and, strangely enough, Peppi was not surprised to hear the horse speak. "I am here to help. I have come a long way and no one has seen me. No one except you, the lowliest one."

THE DONKEY OF GOD

"The lowly shall be exalted," sang Saint Catherine, while Pegasus took up the response.

"The lowly shall go high," he echoed. "High . . ."

Peppi rubbed his eyes. Saint Catherine and Pegasus had vanished; the cave was the stable again. But Peg seemed to be looking at him with a new expression and the sound of the response was still in the boy's ears. "High—go high!" Those were the words. They were not only a promise; they were a command. Peppi knew now what it was he must do.

"Well!" cried Bennuccio as Peppi burst into the bakery. "Has a tempest broken loose? Have you been bewitched from the sad-faced youngster of an hour ago to a prince of the realm? What has happened and where are you going?"

"I haven't time to tell you what's happened," gasped Peppi. "But I'll tell you where I'm going. I'm going to the Council."

Now it was the baker's turn to gasp. "To the Council!" he whispered as a bull might whisper. "In Heaven's name!"

"Yes," said Peppi. "In Heaven's name."

"The boy's gone mad," said Bennuccio to no one in particular. "But madmen must be protected. So if you're really going to the Council, I might as well go with you. Here, Gino"—he called to his helper—"watch the shop for a bit. I'll be back in a few minutes."

THE HORSE OF SIENA

But it was dusk before the three Councillors heard the boy's strange request.

" Let me see if we understand it correctly," said the youngest of the three, though not one was young. " This boy—named Peppi—says his brother Fabio, who is the jockey of the Snail ward, has disappeared. This citizen "—he indicated Bennuccio —" has given us to understand that the missing party has been seen in a resort of the Tortoises. Drunk, I suppose."

" Oh, no, your Lordship," interrupted Peppi. " Fabio must have been taken ill. Fabio wouldn't—at such a time—"

" At all events," continued the Councillor, " the boy claims to have had a vision which directed him here."

" An uncommon occurrence," murmured the second Councillor. " But not an impossible one. And what further ? "

" Further, the boy pleads that he be permitted to represent his ward and ride in his brother's stead."

" That is not usual," said the second Councillor. " But it was done in the palio of 1410. How old is the lad ? "

Peppi knew that jockeys had to be fifteen or over and was about to say " Fifteen," when something within him prompted the truth.

" Twelve years old," he said.

" That is several years lower than the lowest limit," said the first Councillor, doubtfully. " And the course is dangerous."

" If the boy has been guided by a true vision," argued the

second Councillor, " he will be protected. Every course has its dangers. Who speaks for the boy?"

" I speak for him," answered Bennuccio. " He is a brave lad. As you see, my lords, he is hard-pressed. But he never complains; he never asks special consideration. For that reason he deserves it—though it is bold of me to put it that way."

" I, too, speak for him," said Pieró, whom Bennuccio had sent for. " We poets are supposed to have the gift of second-sight, yet I know the lad's vision is purer than mine. I have watched him for years and never have I found a fault in him."

There was a silence in the ceremonial chamber; Peppi seemed smaller than ever in the great hall. Presently the first Councillor spoke.

" It is against all rules of the palio," he said. " It is no race for children."

" But he is not a child," the second Councillor urged. " Has he not taken care of a brother six years older than himself? And does not that entitle him to a ranking beyond his years?"

Again silence lay heavy in the enormous room, and the two Councillors turned to their senior. Throughout the discussion the third Councillor had not spoken a word. Now he rose and uttered three short sentences.

" The boy Peppi shall represent the ward of the Snail. The horse he has tended shall be ridden by him in the palio tomorrow. It is his right."

THE HORSE OF SIENA

Then he left the room, the others following.

That evening Siena was a feast of lights. No one would have recognised the plaza as the daily market-place; the booths, walled with branches and roofed with canvas, were gone. Tar-barrels blazed on top of each other; red and green fires made the scene vivid as noon and twice as colourful. Boys in every ward had burning sticks that twirled and spouted stars. Bonfires in the streets were reflected in the skies and answered by flares on the surrounding hills. Only the ward of the Snail did not join in the merry-making; a few candles were all that burned in that section of the city. But there was a light in Peppi's heart as he went to sleep, a light that burned more steadily than any torch.

The citizens of the Snail had gone to bed with despair; they woke with anger. Their enemies had piled insult upon injury. Treachery was at work again; one of the guards must have been bribed to let in a band of Tortoises during the night, for the Snails found their church had been defiled. The steps, the pillars, the very sides of the building were foul with slimy tracks; and—to make the insult worse—the tracks were made by snails—the smallest and ugliest snails imaginable. It was all the citizens could do to remove the creatures before the services began.

It had gotten about that Peppi was to ride Peg for the ward, and, though no one had any hope of victory, it was agreed

THE DONKEY OF GOD

that no part of the ceremony should be left out. Accordingly, Peppi, leading Peg, was allowed to go ahead of the others who thronged to the church. When the doors were opened, Peppi—and Peg—were led up the steps.

At the foot of the high altar, the priest was waiting. He was dressed in his richest surplice; his stole was embroidered in seed-pearls. All the other members wore their finest costumes. Though the Snails were one of the poorest wards, the people brought out their best, and here and there some family relic drew the eye; a clasp or a carved helmet shone as proudly as it did when a prince wore it.

Peppi advanced. Peg followed. Up to the altar, boy and horse walked among the rows of silent men and singing candles. Every one knelt except the horse and the priests. Prayers were said—Peppi said an extra " Ave " and remembered Saint Eloy, patron saint of horse-shoers—and the benediction began.

" Lord, hear this prayer and let my cry come to thee."

" *Oremus*," came the response. " Let us pray."

" Lord, we beseech thee, that we . . ."

Peppi could not understand the words. While the priest was intoning the syllables, Peppi was whispering to Peg and, possibly, to himself, " Don't be afraid. The saints will help us, especially Saint Catherine. And Pegasus will be with us. Don't be afraid."

THE HORSE OF SIENA

The priest had reached the end of the blessing.

" Let this animal have thy favour, O Lord. May it be preserved in body and kept free from harm. Let it receive thy blessing. . . . Amen."

Then, as the people echoed " Amen," the priest sprinkled holy water over the horse, a few drops fell on Peppi's forehead, and the service was over.

An hour later no one was in any of the seventeen wards. All Siena was wedged along the shell-shaped course that bordered the plaza. The centre of the plaza was like a bowl, slightly flattened on one side, and it was on the rim of this stony basin that the palio would be run. But that would not happen for some time yet. Meanwhile the crowd amused itself with what was going on in the middle of the bowl.

First there was a mock bull-fight, in which the bulls and horses were human beings and the riders were repeatedly thrown, to the immense delight of the onlookers. Sometimes the forelegs of one of the animals would quarrel with the hindlegs, which was comic enough; but when the brown cloth, which represented the hide, split in two and hind-legs would take forelegs by the throat, the crowd screamed with laughter. Then a short *calcio* was played, the *calcio* being something

THE DONKEY OF GOD

like American football only rougher (if possible!) and with twenty-seven instead of eleven players on each side. This occupied another exciting hour until the banner of the winning Dragon was hoisted.

Peppi saw none of this, for he was waiting with his *contrada* in one of the little streets that led into the plaza. Then the warning-bell rang from the tower, the trumpets spoke three times, and the procession began.

First came two heralds with the black and white arms of Siena swinging from long silver bugles. Then came archers who shot bright-coloured ribbons into the crowd; and fortunate were they who caught them, for at the ends were little parcels that contained a cake or a cap or a toy or some other surprise.

These were followed by a group of jugglers and clowns who made the people lose their breath between wonder and merriment. And then the parade itself, with every ward trying to outdo the other. Each ward had its own standard-bearer, but he did far more than merely carry the banner. The standard-bearer was really a high-class juggler, for the chief part of his performance was tossing his flag high in the air, revolving it about his neck, passing it between his legs, sliding it down his back, trailing it within an inch of the ground, and then shooting it twenty feet in the air—all of this without losing the beat of the music and always keeping his colours unfurled.

THE HORSE OF SIENA

Each ward had its own drummers, as well; its own escorts who led the *contrada's* horse; and its own pages who attended the wagons or floats. These decorated wagons drew the most attention, for each one told the story of its war—or explained its name—and each year they were different.

This year the first to enter the plaza was the ward of the Goose. Last year the wagon and its attendants illustrated the legend of The Goose Who Laid the Golden Eggs, but this year it told another story. The float was built up high to represent a hill, on top of which was a fort with sleeping sentries at the gates; and on the highest battlement were three live—and loud-lunged—geese. Every one understood this represented the night when sleeping Rome was attacked by the invaders, and the cackling of the geese roused the sentries and saved the city. When the float, drawn by four horses, was in front of the reviewing-stand with the Councillors and nobles, the geese cackled louder than ever, the sentries sprang up, the gates flew open, and a Roman general—made up as Manlius, in golden breastplate and plumed helmet—appeared, announced his victory and made a speech. He told how, after the invaders were defeated, the geese had wandered south, were lost in the hills, and finally reached Siena, where their feathers made beds for the poor people to lie on and their quills became the pens of poets. The part of Manlius was performed by one of the most popular poets, and when he finished

THE DONKEY OF GOD

his speech—which was all in rhyme—the spectators applauded and cried " Bravo ! "

The second group in the procession was that of the Owl. All the attendants were dressed in long gowns and peaked caps, for they represented wise men and scholars. Their car was built like a classic monument with steps around it. On these steps were grouped living statues of scholars and philosophers, and on the highest step was a figure, representing Minerva, the goddess of wisdom, with the owl on her shoulder. The attendants distributed a poem which related how Minerva's bird had chosen their ward and how Siena was now sure of having wise councillors and protectors.

Then came the ward of the Dragon, headed by a military band. Last year their float pictured Saint George and his famous encounter, but this year it celebrated the story of Cadmus, the Greek hero. Cadmus was shown, having killed the dragon, obeying the command to sow the dragon's teeth and water them with its blood. When the wagon arrived at the Councillor's stand, there was a sudden burst of music and, where the teeth had been planted, soldiers sprang up—as in the fable—fully-armed. With the sun flashing from their armour, they went through a military drill, while Cadmus—the poet of the Dragons—explained how the soldiers had migrated to his ward, and how, since they were nurtured by dragon's blood, they would be bold as dragons in combat, glad to give their blood whenever Siena was in danger.

THE HORSE OF SIENA

The She-Wolf followed. Its outfit was simpler, but it was received with the greatest enthusiasm. No sonnets were distributed, no poet was needed to explain. Even the children knew that a she-wolf had mothered the twins Romulus and Remus; that Romulus had founded Rome, which bore his name; and that Remus had brought his son, who was ill, into the Tuscan hills. There he was restored to health and the son, whose name was Senus, established the city of Siena. The float was divided in two parts: one half displayed the mother-wolf suckling the two babes; the other half showed Senus laying the first stones of Siena. The flag-bearer was the most daring of the lot. His head and shoulders covered in a wolf's skin, he turned somersaults with the flag in one hand, executed difficult dance-steps, threw the banner far ahead of him and caught it before its fringes could touch the ground.

And so the procession went on. The richer wards had elaborate displays, the poorer ones more modest. The Giraffe contributed an enormous wagon decorated with palms and bamboo to resemble a jungle in which hunters had captured a live giraffe. The Unicorn had little except a milk-white stallion with a pasteboard pointed horn attached to its forehead. But, rich or poor, every ward had its emblem, its standard-bearer and its decorated wagon.

All except the Snail. This ward was so poor that it could only afford a few pages to accompany its emblem-bearer and he was none of the best. Tossing the banner with its gold snail

THE DONKEY OF GOD

on a green ground, he stumbled and let it fall—and the crowd jeered. The Tortoises were loudest in their scorn.

" Yah ! " they called. " Snails may carry their house on their backs but they can't carry their own flag ! Yah ! "

But Peppi, in a helmet three sizes too large for him, did not flinch. " Don't let them frighten you," he said to Peg—or was it to himself ?—" Noise isn't going to stop us, and waving flags won't win races." He bent over and stroked Peg's long neck. So, without glory but without any other mishaps, they passed the reviewing-stand. Then the parade disbanded ; there was an intermission for rest and refreshments ; and the track was made ready for the chief event.

It was late in the afternoon when the ten horses were strung out, more or less evenly, at the starting-post. Peppi was crowded to the outermost rim and, once there, he was forgotten. The other jockeys stood up in their stirrups with excitement for they knew what was to come. A bell clanged, the rope fell, and the short whips came down. But most of the blows did not fall on the backs of the horses, but on the jockeys' ! Instead of whipping up their steeds, they began flogging each other. Two of the jockeys were locked in what seemed a death-grip ; two were actually wrestling ; two others

THE HORSE OF SIENA

were pummelling each other's faces while their horses broke through the crowd and ran away down a side-street. The spectators yelled with delight, screamed with surprise, jumped in the air, beat on each other's shoulders, howled, stamped, cursed, and encouraged the jockeys to greater blows. It was more like a battle than a horse-race.

Meanwhile, Peppi had escaped the worst. Because of his age and his poor position on the outside of the track, no one had paid any attention to him. Besides, his horse was such a queerly built beast that the other jockeys did not take him seriously. " That bone-pile in a race ? " sneered the jockey of the Tortoises. " He'll be lucky if he can crawl half way round —and by that time we'll be finishing the third lap ! "

Peg and Peppi actually were half way round before the other jockeys were even aware of it. Six of them, still punishing each other, spurred their horses and were after the boy.

" Now, Peg, we must show them ! " cried Peppi. " Now, Peg ! Now ! " His whip hung useless in his hand ; he could not bear to use it. Words were his only spurs. " Come, Peg ! Remember what we must do ! That's right ! Now gallop ! Good Peg ! Keep it up ! Up ! Up ! "

Peg was doing his best. But the six jockeys were gaining fast. At the dangerous turn opposite the Governor's palace, two of them caught up with him, and Peg, rounding the corner

THE DONKEY OF GOD

at the end of the first lap, stumbled. In a moment all six were beside him and a shower of blows pelted the scrawny back and thin sides. Peg staggered and sank to his knees. Peppi saved himself only by holding fast to the horse's neck. The six jockeys passed him one after the other.

"Holy Saint Catherine," cried Peppi. "Do not forsake us now. Lend us your strength. Pegasus—hear me! Help me!"

Then something happened. Just what, Peppi never knew. The horse's back suddenly seemed to straighten; his neck grew firm; his hooves struck the paved ground like thunder. Then Peppi felt a great wind in his face. For the next few minutes it was as if he were being hurled through a dream—a dream of flying. The world became a huge, humming top. The faces in the crowd spun around, faster, faster. And faster Peppi flew. Now the first jockey was being passed; now the second, now the third . . . the wind blew wilder . . . the fourth. The other two were still far in the lead. But Peg was creeping up—no, sweeping up—on them. It seemed to Peppi that Peg's feet never touched the stones of the race-track. He was somehow aware that they were on the third lap—the last lap—of the course and that they were already abreast of the fifth jockey. Passed. Faster . . . Now the sixth—and even before he could finish his thought the sixth was behind them. Faster . . . No one was near them now. They finished in a flying cloud of dust, whirling past the winning-post so many

THE HORSE OF SIENA

lengths ahead of the nearest horse that no one counted. All Siena went wild!

Peppi did not see his triumph. He did not witness how the crowds surged into the bowl, rushing from every part of the plaza. He did not watch his ward-companions stretch their hands and catch the silver cup and silk banner which the Councillors lowered to them. He was not aware that Piero had lifted him to the shoulders of Bennuccio, and that the members of the Snail were half caressing, half carrying their horse to the church where he was blessed a second time. Peppi had fainted.

Nor could Peppi remember the events of that night. As in a dream, he felt himself borne from street to street, toasted at every corner, praised, kissed, loaded with presents, wept over and almost worshipped. Later, in the best part of the Snail ward, a long table was set up in the open street and every one was invited to share. Bennuccio had baked a hundred small breads, twelve pies and a towering iced cake for the occasion. Peppi—as becomes a hero—was at one end of the table; Peg—as was only his right—was at the other. And everything the others had, even wine and spaghetti, the horse had, too.

While every one was feasting and singing, Peppi slipped off to one side where Piero was sitting with a strange expression in his eyes.

THE DONKEY OF GOD

" Tell me," said Peppi.

" What can I tell ? " said the poet. " You and I are the only ones who know what happened—and even we cannot be sure. Was it really Peg you rode on or—the other one ? I know, better than most, that the gods disguise themselves when they come to earth. But who can recognise the divine spark in a bag of bones ? "

" But didn't you see ? " asked Peppi.

" There was too much dust," said Piero. " Besides," he added after a moment, " a poet's eyes are likely to play tricks on him. I can swear I saw your awkward Peg begin the race. Yet—when he passed me—it was not the same horse. There were wings, unearthly wings, in the plaza to-day ; the air shone with them. And when at the end, I lifted you off, I found this in my hand. Look ! It still shines."

Peppi looked. It was a quill-feather.

FLORENCE

FLORENCE

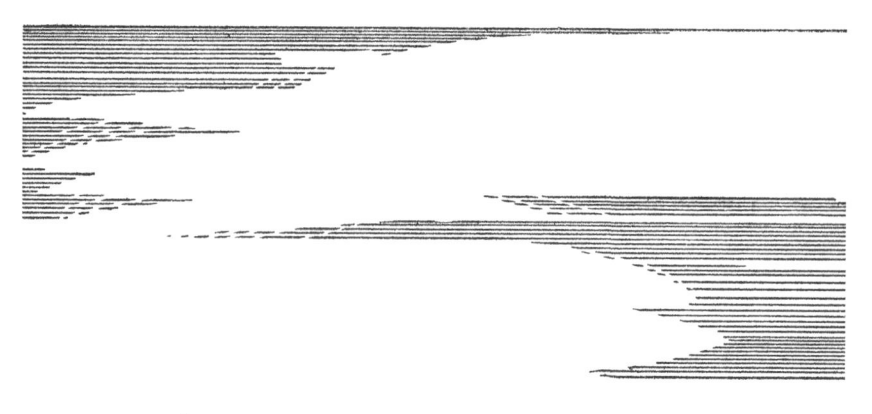

FLORENCE

FLORENCE, the flowering, comes by its name naturally. It was formerly called Fiorenza (Firenze is the modern Italian name) from the Latin Florentia—and, judging from its abundance of blossoms, it is still Flora's city. But Florence, though it has a town's boundaries, is not merely a city; it is a world. Since the Middle Ages, Florence has been an intellectual and artistic centre; it would take pages merely to list its authors, painters and scientists. Its high position was established by the poet Dante (Alighieri), born in Florence in 1265, and here, even when Rome was at its peak, could be found students from furthest lands. Florence was the home of the story-teller Boccaccio whose " Decameron " (a collection of tales told by a group of people staying in Fiesole, a suburb of Florence) was the model for Chaucer's " The Canterbury Tales." Among other famous Florentines were Giotto, who was the father of one of the first great schools of painting; the sculptor Ghiberti, whose bronze doors on the Baptistery in 1402 mark the beginning of the Renaissance; Luca della

THE DONKEY OF GOD

Robbia, the inventor of glazed and coloured terra-cotta, the delicacy of whose medallions has never been surpassed; Donatello, the man who influenced sculpture even more than Michelangelo, who also resided here for a period; Benvenuto Cellini, the jeweller-sculptor; such painters—to name only a few—as Botticelli, Gozzoli, Filippo Lippi, Ghirlandaio, Fra Angelico, the Luca della Robbia of painters; and dozens of others. Their stories have been told a hundred times; the libraries are full of them.

Nor will I go into detail about the public sights, the buildings, the starred " attractions." " Guide-book Florence "—the Florence so carefully charted for those who travel by the book and a checking pencil—lists forty-three museums and galleries, sixty-five palaces, and the Lord knows how many churches and chapels. (Sometimes I think even He must lose track of some of them.) A few of these are, of course, imperative; they are in the class of things you " simply *must* see." You will be lucky if you are not dragged to see them all! But you will be unlucky if you do not see one or two of the popular festivals that need no knowledge of art, literature or history—only a love for the picturesque . . . and for crowds. I am thinking especially of Befana. Befana is the Feast of Epiphany, which means little or nothing to us. But to the Italian—and particularly to the Italian child—it means everything; it is his Fourth of July, his New Year and his Christmas (which is scarcely noticed in Italy) all in one. It takes place on the sixth of January, and on that day masqueraders parade, horns are blown, streets are gay with candles and confetti; every one exchanges kisses and presents. Instead of Santa Claus, there is the mythical Old Woman who comes to good children as a gift-bearing godmother and to naughty children as an ill-favoured, bad-tempered witch.

Then there is Good Friday, when you can witness a procession in ancient Roman costumes; and the Festival of Saint John, on June twenty-fourth, when not only beacon-fires may be seen on the hills, but fireworks in the cathedral square; and Ascension Day when there are more fireworks and every one goes out at dawn to the Cascine (the park laid out by the Medici) and breakfasts on the grass; and the " Scoppio del Carro," or " The Explosion of the Car " which needs a paragraph or two for itself.

On Holy Saturday, the Saturday before Easter, an antique covered car (by courtesy, a chariot) is slowly drawn by four white oxen through the streets of Florence until it reaches the Baptistery, the oldest house of worship in Florence. There it rests. Meanwhile, in the great cathedral directly opposite, preparations have been made which date back to the First Crusade in the Eleventh Century. When Jerusalem was captured by the Crusaders, a young Florentine was the first to plant the Christian flag on the hallowed walls. As a reward

THE DONKEY OF GOD

for his bravery he was given three pieces of rock from the Holy Sepulchre in which Jesus had been entombed. The story goes that when he returned home, he presented the three bits of stone to the Archbishop of Florence and, as soon as the pieces touched the altar, sparks flew between them. The Archbishop immediately lit the holy tapers with the sparks, then the candles, then the great lamps. Ever since that time, the flints have been preserved in the treasury and are used only to light the new fire on Easter Eve.

Now all is ready for the climax. A wire has been stretched from the high altar in the cathedral to the covered car; on the wire rests a rocket shaped like the dove which carried good tidings to Noah. It is noon. In their excitement, the waiting crowds lose what breath they still have and the leaping bells lose all sense of count. As the choir breaks into the *Gloria in Excelsis*, the dove-rocket is ignited from a candle that has been lit by fire from the sacred flints. The fuse sputters, the rocket balances itself a moment, and then the dove soars from the altar, out into the square, and straight toward the " chariot." Down it shoots, and, as it touches the car, flames fly in every direction. The car has been crammed with bombs and fireworks, so it is little wonder that one explosion follows another while the crowds shout their delight.

It is no mere childish pleasure in noise for its own sake that holds the crowd. According to local belief, much depends on how the dove behaves. If everything goes on schedule and the dove returns smoothly to the altar, the harvest will be good and households will be happy; if there is a mishap or even a hitch, the peasants fear the worst for their crops and for themselves.

" Of course," said a Florentine friend who had studied at Cambridge and had married an American, " it's just an old superstition and no sensible man would believe in it to-day. Just the same, I remember what happened a few years ago Instead of shooting across the square, the dove wobbled on its wire and stopped shortly after it left the high altar. A priest had to start it along again, but it scarcely touched the car. Instead of the usual cheerful explosions, there were only fizzes and sputterings, while the dove jerked and fluttered back to the cathedral. Of course it was only a coincidence," said he, shrugging his shoulders. " But I must admit that year half the olives refused to ripen, the potatoes were wormy, the wine was sour, and—worst of all—the crop of tourists was the poorest since the war."

No matter how little or how long you stay in Florence, there are, so every one will insist, five sights that *must* be seen. They are (1) the Cathedral and its Campanile, (2) the priceless bronze doors of the Baptistery, (3) the Piazza della Signoria, the Place of the Governors, (4) the interior of Santa Croce, (5) the twin art museums : the Uffizi and the Pitti Galleries.

THE DONKEY OF GOD

I have no quarrel with this choice, which seems to be unanimously recommended by all the guides and guide-books. The cathedral is a glory in delicate tones—at sunset the rose-coloured marble glows with a double and deeper pink. Its dome, which dates from 1431 and took Brunelleschi fourteen years to build, is unsurpassed even by the sister-dome at Saint Peter's in Rome; its high altar of pure silver was worked over by the greatest artisans for a hundred years; the famous choir-gallery by Donatello is matched by the even more beautiful one by Luca della Robbia, the two pieces comprising the loveliest records of singing and dancing children that have ever been sculptured. The campanile, or bell-tower, designed by Giotto in 1334 when he was architect of the cathedral, is both simple and sumptuous. Its four sides are covered with reliefs (drawn by Giotto and carved by Pisano) showing the beginnings of man, his inventions, his laws, his sciences, his fine and household arts, his conquests of the earth and elements—in short, a parable of man's life and his place among the immensities.

The bronze doors of the Baptistery enclose one of the oldest structures in Italy—the structure, now dedicated to peace, having been raised on the stones of what used to be a temple to Mars, the god of war. The mosaics which crown the interior of the Baptistery are gigantic and gorgeous (if you can see them in the half-dusk inside); the pavement is equally elab-

FLORENCE

orate, with its lace-like patterns of the Zodiac which inspired the designs of the Florentine weavers. But it is the famous bronze doors before which every one gasps. The first pair of doors (completed by Pisano in 1336) represents scenes from the life of John the Baptist; the second and third pair were executed by Ghiberti after a competition in which even the great Brunelleschi was defeated. The second doors, divided into twenty-eight sections, portray episodes in the life of Jesus; the third and most magnificent of the double doors represent ten events from the Old Testament. No one yet has described the majestic quality of these masterpieces although countless attempts have been made—Michelangelo gave some indication of their glory when he said that Ghiberti's doors were "worthy to be the gates of Heaven."

The Piazza della Signoria is not only the most picturesque plaza in Florence but the most art-crowded square in the world. It used to be the Forum of the Republic; the fanatic reformer Savonarola's "pyramid of vanities" was erected and burned here; and here, a year later, the body of the same preacher was burned to ashes. Here occurred so many tragedies, the cruel end of so many feuds, that the ground still seems blood-soaked to the imagination. Here stands the Palazzo Vecchio, the old fortress which housed the governors and city-fathers, crammed with lore and legends. Here, across the narrow alley, is the entrance to the Uffizi Gallery, with its four thousand paint-

THE DONKEY OF GOD

ings, and the connecting rooms in the Pitti Palace—the two forming one of the world's greatest art collections. Here is the Loggia dei Lanzi, a hall from which the rulers used to address the people, but to which the people now come to inspect the sculptures and bronzes. Statues, reproductions of which are in the furthest corners of the world, are everywhere in this piazza: Donatello's dramatic " Judith and Holofernes," Michelangelo's beautifully poised and youthful " David," Giambolognas' vigorous " Rape of the Sabines," and Benvenuto Cellini's masterpiece, " Perseus with the Head of Medusa."

He stands there, this Perseus, as calm as though he had not rescued the loveliest maiden from the loathliest monster. Resting on one foot, the other knee pointed, all of youthful assurance is in that casual pose and its careless strength. Were it not for the curved sword in one hand and the snake-crowned head held up in the other, Perseus might be any young boy standing in a Greek god's shoes. So quietly does Perseus stand it is hard to believe that he was created in a fury of fret and fever.

Cellini, in his autobiography, gives us a complete if highly coloured account of the completion of this bronze. He knew that " Perseus " would be his master-work and he had constructed a special type of furnace to take the mould. He had filled the smelting pot with pieces of copper and tin and other alloys for making bronze, and had arranged the pot so that the metal, when properly heated, should run into the mould. Then, aching with fatigue, he lay down for a short rest, leaving his assistants at their posts. An hour later one of the assistants waked Cellini to tell him there was not enough heat, the metal would neither fuse nor run, and the statue was ruined. Raging, Cellini leaped from his couch, striking those who tried to restrain or console him. He worked, he says, as though supplied with ten arms; he fed the furnace with oak, whipped up the flames, added more metal, put his very breath into the bellows. The room swam in heat; the fire mounted so swiftly that the cap of the furnace blew up. To make matters worse, the workshop took fire and, to increase the confusion, a storm broke in tempestuous lightnings. The wind howled; the workmen screamed; Cellini outroared them all. The rain put the fires out and the furnace was plugged up. Somehow, the statue was shaped and the metal fused, although it needed more tin. There was no time to send for more. Cellini scoured the house, threw pewter jugs into the boiling metal, pewter plates, jars, dishes—two hundred of them, he says—until the mould was filled to the last crevice. Then, throwing himself on his knees, he gave thanks to God and sank into unconsciousness. When he woke, the fever was gone and the statue finished in its perfection.

A year later, in 1554, his " Perseus " was unveiled in the Loggia dei Lanzi where it now stands. All art-loving and fash-

THE DONKEY OF GOD

ionable Florence was there. Poets hung their sonnets on the pillars, musicians composed songs in its honour, even Cellini's rivals forgot their jealousies and outdid each other in admiration. Cellini, dressed in elaborate finery, walked among them, one hand cavalierly resting on the hilt of his sword, drinking in their praises like the spoiled artist he was. He did not suffer from too much modesty. He believed that his creation was unsurpassed and even unsurpassable. And, looking at his " Perseus " to-day, who can say he was wrong?

The church of Santa Croce, which I have already referred to, is known as " the Pantheon of Florence," just as the real Pantheon is known as " the Westminster Abbey of Rome." The reason for the designation lies in the fact that Santa Croce contains the tombs and monuments of so many of the most celebrated Italians. Here is the memorial to the poet Dante, here lie the architect-sculptor-painter Michelangelo, the literary statesman Machiavelli, the scientist Galileo, and other great ones. Santa Croce also contains the story of the Holy Cross (hence its name), embodied in a set of murals painted by Gaddi; two magnificent series of frescoes by Giotto at his purest and best, illustrating scenes from the lives of Saint Francis and Saint John the Evangelist; and the adjoining clois-

FLORENCE

ters, two colonnades which, denying their simple aims, are more like palatial courts.

But, impressive though Santa Croce undoubtedly is, I prefer two somewhat smaller churches: Santa Maria Novella and San Lorenzo. Santa Maria Novella makes an instant appeal, not because it is " the purest and most elegant example of Tuscan Gothic," but because every inch of it is precious. If it held nothing else, it would be glorious on account of the decorated choir, the most important work of Ghirlandaio. Four years, it is said, were spent before the paintings were completed, during which time Ghirlandaio was assisted by a young pupil named Michelangelo. It is a striking work, striking in idea as well as execution. And it is a daring one, mingling the time of Jesus with the time of the Medici, the paintings having been finished in the very year when an obscure sailor from Genoa, one Cristoforo Colombo, set sail for what he thought was India. For example, the painter shows us the birth of the Virgin—and, as the child is being washed, the artist introduces Lodovica Tornabuoni, the daughter of Florence's leading banker in 1492 (the chief business street is still called after him) and four court ladies. Into the humble room of John the Baptist comes the richly dressed Ginevra de' Benci, the great beauty of Ghirlandaio's days. The scenes in the Temple are made livelier by the introduction of politicians, bankers—and the artist himself!

THE DONKEY OF GOD

The Cappella degli Spagnuoli (Spanish Chapel) has a most elaborate, completely decorated set of designs which have been praised by Ruskin—in two chapters of his " Mornings in Florence "—and other scholars. I must confess that I can make little of the story—it is all extremely allegorical—but the design pleases me as music does. One listens to the unfolding of sweet sounds without asking what they *mean*; so here, I am willing to watch colours and figures mount heavenward without asking what message they bear. Even the huge " Paradise " by Orcagna in the adjacent chapel needs no explanation. The mood of quiet grandeur, of singing silence, a music unheard, is all we know " and all we need to know."

But the crucifix by Brunelleschi in Santa Maria Novella is another thing. I cannot describe it, but some idea of its wasted beauty may be obtained if I repeat the story of how it came to be carved.

The two sculptors, Donatello and Brunelleschi were good friends. Donatello was already the more famous, so when he exhibited his crucifix his rival was embarrassed.

" Speak up, man," cried Donatello. " What do you think of it ? "

" Oh, Master," replied Brunelleschi, " you are so much

greater than I that any opinion from me would be an impertinence."

But Donatello, seeing his friend was trying to evade his question, would not be put off. "Come, come," he urged, "I really want your judgment—frankly. Tell me just what you're thinking."

"Well," stammered the younger man, "I was thinking that your Christ wasn't very Christ-like, that he looked like—" he gulped, then blurted out—" like a peasant."

Donatello, in spite of his greatness, was hurt. "It's all right to criticise," he grumbled. "But criticism would be more effective if you could do better than the object you ridicule."

Some time later, Brunelleschi invited the master to lunch. They bought provisions on their way to the studio; Brunelleschi bearing the wine, Donatello carrying the eggs and vegetables in his apron. When they entered the studio—Donatello ahead—the first thing to be seen was a newly carved crucifix around which the noonday sun threw a nimbus of light.

Donatello threw up his hands, forgetting the lunch-filled apron. "Mother of God!" he whispered, staring at the shrunken limbs, the limp body, the tragically bowed head. Then, looking down at the litter of vegetables and broken eggs, he added ruefully, "You were right, Brunelleschi. I am a clumsy wood-chopper. Compared to this, my Christ is a peasant—and the work of a peasant!"

THE DONKEY OF GOD

I have hinted that the church of San Lorenzo is even more interesting than Santa Croce. The outside is flatly disappointing: it lacks a face. This is the more strange since San Lorenzo is the earliest cathedral of Florence. It was consecrated as early as 393, rebuilt in 1410; and in 1515 Leo X gave Michelangelo the order to make a façade which was to be the most impressive in Europe. That was over four hundred years ago—and the façade is still missing.

But, though Michelangelo's differences with Popes and potentates prevented him from carrying out his most ambitious schemes, they did not prevent him from creating, if not completing, the world's most inspiring chapel. The rest of the church has little of interest, except two bronze pulpits which represent Donatello's last work. But the so-called "New Sacristy" (better known as the Medici Chapel) is never to be forgotten. It is colossal in scope, overpowering in effect. The room itself, a great cube surmounted by a dome, has the severity of some unearthly resting-place—a god's mausoleum—as though the world's problems were entombed here. The solemnity is emphasised by Michelangelo's tombs, the tombs of the two Medici princes, with their contrasting figures. Giuliano, sitting erect with baton in his hand, can be interpreted as the General of the Church, or Commander of the Army, or the Man of Action, energetic even in repose. Lorenzo, meditating with finger pressed against the lip, is his opposite:

FLORENCE

Lorenzo is the Dreamer, the absorbed Visionary; the deep intensity of his shadowed expression has earned him the name of " Il Penseroso " (" The Thinker ").

Yet, in spite of their majesty, it is not the monuments themselves nor the figures of the two princes which impress us most. What one remembers longest are the four figures—two on each sarcophagus—four statues whose nobility is matched by their mystery. Michelangelo never gave them names, but they are commonly supposed to represent Night and Day, Twilight and Dawn. They are not happy figures. Dawn, usually pictured as laughing, young and " rosy-fingered," is here a woman raising herself with an effort as though she feared to face the day. Twilight is a man sorrowfully contemplating the world between light and darkness. Here Night is sunk in her own despair. Even Day is gloomy. Instead of being a shining presence, he is a labouring giant rising unwillingly from his bed of stone; like rock parting from rock.

No, they are not happy figures. But it must be remembered, Michelangelo was not happy when he made them. His mind was full of the siege of Florence, his country's fate and the loss of liberty, as well as with his private quarrels. The figure of Night (said to be his favourite statue) is the one which has attracted most admirers. Swinburne wrote a splendid sonnet (" In San Lorenzo") which begins, " Is thine hour come to wake, O slumbering Night ? " and even in Michelangelo's time

THE DONKEY OF GOD

it caught the attention of poets. One of them by the name of Strozzi wrote some lines which might be translated:

> Yes, this is Night—the Night we all must seek—
> A sleeping rock. But since an Angel[1] gives
> This rock a soul, she sleeps, she breathes, she lives.
> You doubt it ? Wake her then—and she will speak.

To which Michelangelo, thinking of his country's wrongs, replied as though the statue had been given a voice:

> I am content to sleep in stone, while hot
> Rage and betrayal war on bloody ground.
> I am content to sleep and hear no sound.
> So pass by, stranger. Whisper—wake me not.

San Marco was originally a monastery, but is now a museum; once a home for Dominican monks, it has become a shrine for Fra Angelico. I have already spoken of this pious painter whose work was so devout that he was called " the Blessed "; a mere glance inside San Marco is enough to show the reason. The chapter-house, the cloisters, the corridors, even the cells were decorated so that Angelico's brother-worshippers would have objects of devotion in private as well as in public. (The cell once occupied by Savonarola contains relics of that preacher-reformer.) Italy is crammed with Last Judgments,

[1] A play on the name of the sculptor Angelo, which is Italian for " angel."

FLORENCE

Descents from the Cross, Annunciations, Presentations and Coronations of the Virgin—yet Fra Angelico has taken these well-worn subjects and treated them as though they had never been painted before. The colouring is pure, the expressions are glorified; devotion and humility are in every line of the reverent hands, in every fold of the angels' garments. When Angelico painted Christ upon the cross it is said that he wept as loud as though he had assisted at the Crucifixion.

Another legend concerns the " Annunciation," possibly Angelico's most admired work. He had, so the story goes, reached the last stage of his radiant fresco. The kneeling angel, with wings that had brushed the rainbow still quivering, was about to deliver his message; the Virgin, with clasped hands, was waiting to receive it. But the space that should have contained the features of the Virgin was empty. Try as he would, Angelico found he could not paint the adored and adorable face. His drawings were cast aside; nothing he had ever attempted seemed worthy. It grew dark. Angelico put down his brushes, prayed, and slept. That night he dreamed an angel had entered through the narrow window and taken up his brushes. Angelico, the monk, could scarcely lift his eyes in the presence of the angel; but Angelico, the painter, could not help noticing how the heavenly one mixed his colours. When he woke, it was morning and the first thing Angelico noticed was his transformed palette and his brushes—wet—and with a colour no mortal had ever conceived. Then he looked at his fresco. And there, in a more than earthly glow, was his painting—finished—the face of the Virgin complete to the smallest eyelash, wearing that mixture of modesty and ecstasy which only angels know.

Therefore, the tale concludes, it is only natural that Giovanni da Fiesole should be known as Fra Angelico, the Angelic Brother. For was he not guided by one of the heavenly brotherhood, and was there ever a master who had been pupil to an angel?

Unless you are on the look-out for it, you are likely to miss one of the most remarkable rooms in all Italy. The Palazzo Riccardi (originally the Palazzo Medici) was once an outstanding building, the home of the Medici family for more than a hundred years. That was in the Fifteenth and Sixteenth Centuries. Now the structure, hemmed in by a business district, seems nothing more than a dark grey building, something like a squat fortress and something like a rough-hewn, three-story house that welcomes no one.

Nor is there much to invite you in the interior. The once brilliant court is a bureau for petty government officials; the once gay chambers are now dull offices. You will do well also to skip the gallery with its " sumptuous apartment." In reality

FLORENCE

it is one of the gaudiest salons in existence; a room that looks like a wedding-cake struck by lightning—or Hollywood.

But it is worth ten times your trouble merely to walk inside one little room at the top of the staircase. This was the private chapel of the Medici, and here Benozzo Gozzoli covered the walls with his magnificent " Journey of the Magi." It is, literally, a work of wonder, the more wonderful since the dark chapel originally had no windows, and Gozzoli painted his hundreds of figures by lamplight! (Since then a window and a door have been inserted—right through the painting!) The entire chapel is like a jewelled tapestry or like a set of miniatures magnified to life-size. Gozzoli set out to paint the visit of the Magi—that favourite subject of the three kings journeying to Bethlehem—but he ended by painting a mediaeval pageant which is the finest record of the costumes of that period. Under the guise of the Biblical story, we have a Fifteenth Century procession of princes with hunting-dogs, falcons, trained leopards, squires and pages. The landscape is Tuscan—the castle from which the parade is unwinding is an actual palace near Fiesole—and the retinue is composed of Gozzoli's famous contemporaries. The oldest king is, in reality, Joseph, Patriarch of Constantinople, who is buried in Santa Maria Novella; the second king is John Paleologus, Emperor of the East; the third king is the handsome Lorenzo " the Magnificent," the young heir of the Medici, attended by members of

THE DONKEY OF GOD

his family and the learned men of his day. Here, mounted on a white horse whose trappings bear the Medici coat-of-arms, is Cosimo " the father of his country "; and here are his brothers Lorenzo and Piero " the Gouty," and his second son, Giuliano, and a host of scholars, among whom Gozzoli has placed himself. It is not hard to find the painter; he is wearing a red headgear—and, so that you cannot mistake him, Gozzoli has painted his name jauntily upon his cap.

The fourth wall is scarcely a wall. It is a vision; it leaves the earth and rises straight into Paradise. Here, in a garden lovelier than Eden, a garden of pomegranates and roses, a throng of angels is celebrating the birth of the Saviour. Some of the seraphs are kneeling, some are whispering, some are adoring in silence. And, on Christmas Eve, so runs a tale, when the room is deserted of visitors and even the caretaker has gone home, unearthly voices may be heard singing, " Glory to God in the highest; peace on Earth," while the chapel fills with the fragrance of roses and pomegranates.

Then there is the Bargello, which, in the Thirteenth Century, was a fortress. It became in turn, a prison, the home of the governor, and, later, after being assigned to the head-of-police (the Bargello, from whom it got its name), a house of horrors with a torture-chamber. Now it is a quaint and quiet

FLORENCE

museum of arts and crafts. Its courtyard and outer staircase are lined with tablets and escutcheons of former governors; its armoury (formerly the torture-chamber) contains many royal pieces belonging to the Medici; its collection of coloured terra-cotta reliefs by the Robbia family is the finest in existence. Its sculptures alone, particularly those of Donatello, and most particularly his statues of St. George and St. John, make the Bargello world-renowned.

If there is time you might venture into San Michele to see the extraordinary tabernacle by Orcagna, or into the state apartments of the Pitti Palace, or into the Academy of Fine Arts which, besides the collection of ancient masters (interesting only to students), contains several works by Michelangelo, particularly the original of his heroic " David."

This " David," possibly the most celebrated work of Michelangelo, was executed when the master was still in his twenties and was carved from a gigantic block of marble which had been discarded as too poor to use. When Michelangelo finished his bold statue it was placed in front of the Palazzo Vecchio and won the applause of every one. Every one, that is, except one pompous magistrate who, after praising it cautiously, said, " It's not *quite* right. Of course I'm not an art critic, but—"

" What seems wrong? " asked the sculptor, controlling his temper, which was a rare thing for him to do.

THE DONKEY OF GOD

" Well, if you ask me, the nose is too large."

Gravely mounting a ladder, Michelangelo pretended to chip at the nose of young David, dropping a little marble-dust which was already on his apron.

" How is it now ? " he asked.

" Perfect ! " replied the critic. " I knew it needed something. You couldn't deceive *me* ! "

" No," murmured Michelangelo, with a mocking bow. " No artist can ever throw dust in the eyes of a good critic."

But in spite of its indoor glories, the magic of Florence lies outdoors. If every painting were burned, every palace tumbled, every statue ground to dust, Florence would still breathe the enchantment that makes every visitor long to return. A walk along the Arno proves this. Not that the Arno is anything much in the way of rivers. Compared to the Hudson or the Rhine it is a muddy little trickle. And yet something rises from its banks that always allures, something that is borne down from the surrounding hills and across the old bridges lined with goldsmiths' shops. Distance not only lends enchantment to the view, it duplicates the spell. The " other side " of the Arno widens the panorama. A view down from Bellosguardo or from San Miniato or from the ancient suburb of Fiesole with its Roman theatre, reveals the domes and slender towers of this " Athens of the West " even better than a more intimate aspect.

The streets are no less individual. Here is the house where, in the year 1265, Dante was born; and here, in a neighbouring street, he met his Beatrice. Here, jutting from the heavy stones, are the delicately wrought lanterns and torch-holders of four hundred years ago. And here, in the very heart of the city, is

THE DONKEY OF GOD

the piazza where everything begins and ends, the great square which has witnessed nearly every important happening in Florence. History talks to us again from these stones and marbles; ghosts trail their legends as mysteriously as on the midnights of the Medici. No building has more to tell than the Palazzo Vecchio, the Old Palace, especially of what happened during the rule of that famous and infamous family. It is in this haunted castle that I have placed the story entitled " The Painted Death."

THE PAINTED DEATH

"THE PICTURE!" HE GASPED. "THE PAINTED DEATH!"

THE PAINTED DEATH

THERE were eight of them and they called themselves
"The Deliverers." A few others called them that, also;
but not many, for their organisation was secret. Less than
a handful of citizens of Florence suspected that gentle Lelio,
the young dandy who almost swooned at the sight of blood,
had taken a certain oath, pressing a razor-edged sword to his
naked breast. Or that the fat and waddling Pandolfo, who
never had a thought about anything, had delivered the most
burning speech ever heard by soldiers not easily moved. Or
that the fruit-seller Neri, whose nick-name (" the dark one ")
seemed to refer to his complexion, was really so-called because
of his black hatred for the oppressors.

It was a strange company—if it could be called a company,
for they were scarce seen together. The young noble Prisco,
whose father had owned the Pazzi palace, was one of its most
ardent leaders; but he was neither more intense nor more important than Nanni, the old cheese-monger from Fiesole. Raffaelo, the Pope's grand-nephew, did not even acknowledge

THE DONKEY OF GOD

Taddeo's obeisance when he walked through the market; yet in the underground chamber, none of the eight listened to Taddeo, the butcher, more respectfully than Raffaelo.

Gian was both the youngest and the most mysterious of the conspirators. Even the members of his own group knew little or nothing about him. It was rumoured that he was a distant relation of the very family he was pledged to overthrow; and, though no one knew his occupation, he was always fastidiously dressed, always well supplied with funds. It was Gian who had found the subterranean room in which they met, and it was he who had drawn up their charter, each sentence of which spelled death.

It was, as I have said, a curiously assorted group with many differences and only one thing in common. That one thing was a deep hatred for the Medici family and a resolve that their rule must end. Once a great dynasty, the Medici had become despots who stopped at nothing to maintain their fast-shrinking power. Cosimo, "the father of his country," had been beloved; Lorenzo, "the Magnificent," had made Florence a world-centre; even Piero, "the Gouty," was tolerated since he was an invalid and bore an illustrious name. But Alessandro, the present ruler, was respected by none, feared by most, and hated by all. His origins were uncertain. Some said his mother was descended from the wild Moors and that his father was the town hangman; others claimed that he never

THE PAINTED DEATH

had a mother, but was begotten by the devil himself. Yet, if no one agreed about his parentage, no one disputed the fact that Alessandro " the Moor " was the most vicious tyrant that Florence had ever known. It was common knowledge that he had poisoned his cousin Ippolito, that he had given the order which resulted in the assassination of two Cardinals who had preached against him, and that his first wife had disappeared three months after her dowry had been delivered.

But it was not Alessandro's private sins that were being discussed by the eight Deliverers as they sat in the underground room beneath the old guild-house.

" I say nothing of the wrongs he has committed against individuals," Taddeo was insisting in his thick voice, blunt as one of his own meat-mallets. " For these he will have to answer to his Maker—whoever his Maker may be. It is his crimes against the public that cannot be forgiven. And for these he must answer to us ! "

" As usual, I agree with Taddeo," said the patrician Raffaelo. " I might add that the Moor's chief crime against the public is his mere existence, and," he added in a tone whose lightness did not conceal its intensity, " I for one see no reason for the continuance."

" Alessandro's offences do not grow less," said Lelio mildly, rolling up the document from which he had been reading. " They increase. Executions have become a pastime with him ;

THE DONKEY OF GOD

the most sacred laws are toys for him to break; he sends judges into exile on a whim and puts court-fools in their stead! And we are no nearer our goal than when we met two years ago."

There was a silence. Gian was the only one who had not spoken, and the other seven looked at the youth as he arose. To-night he was dressed entirely in wine-red with a thin black band which made the colour seem still more fiery.

" You have not heard the worst," said Gian, with a peculiar smile. " Two of our agents have reported that Alessandro, realising the danger of his position, is going to turn Florence over to its old enemies. Messengers have already gone to France promising the loot of Tuscany in return for troops. But that is not all. From another source I learn that one of his henchmen suspects our existence. I need not tell you what will happen if that suspicion is confirmed."

Strangely enough, no one seemed surprised. " It was only a question of time," said Prisco, shrugging his handsome shoulders.

" And the next step? " asked Neri, as casually as though he were asking the price of oranges.

" That is," added Raffaelo, " if we are ready to take steps."

" Is there any doubt? " asked Lelio, unable to disguise his eagerness. " Or must we wait for a sign? "

" Here is your sign," said Gian, touching the black band. " And we need wait no longer. I wear this for the first time

THE PAINTED DEATH

to-night, but I shall not take it off until Alessandro sleeps quieter than he has ever slept—and in a deeper bed. This ribbon is the sign of Giovanni of the Black Band, Giovanni whom most Italians know as 'the fearless freebooter.' Freebooter he is, but he is also a Medici—one of the forgotten members—and he comes to Florence partly in answer to our prayers, partly to fulfil his own."

"But our plans?" inquired Lelio.

"Are the same as his," answered Gian. "He comes here to avenge the disgrace of his family. The Deliverers are here to wipe out the dishonour of our city. And, since the two are one in idea, we will unite in action. As you see, I have joined his party in secret; in three days I shall wear the black band in public—in the Palazzo Vecchio."

"What!" shouted Prisco and Nanni in one breath.

"In three days?" exclaimed Raffaelo incredulously.

"Possibly in less," said Gian, with the same peculiar smile. "To-morrow Giovanni the Fearless will approach the city. The soldiers at the west gate will admit him, for they have joined his cause. As he crosses the Arno, two of Alessandro's divisions will thrown down their arms and, shouting, 'Death to the Tyrant!' will pick them up and fall in behind Giovanni's troops. No one will oppose him. The people will rush to welcome him; our own delegations will swell his ranks. You, Raffaelo, will answer for the priests; you, Prisco, for the patricians; and you, Nanni, for the market-people. None will remain loyal to Alessandro except his mercenaries. By the time the crowds reach the palace-square, it will be no trouble to overpower his handful. And then—!"

Gian did not finish his sentence. None of the eight Deliverers felt it was necessary.

A day passed without event, but there was the same tightness in the air that precedes an electric storm. The heavens seemed full of unheard thunder; the streets tingled with explosive rumours. That day Duke Alessandro did not leave his palace.

The following morning, Giovanni's black-banded soldiers approached the chief gate of Florence and were admitted by Alessandro's guards as simply as though they were peasants on market-day—even more simply, since they did not have to pay the usual entry tax. At the second bridge two hundred horsemen disputed the way; but it was only a show of resistance, and, before a drop of blood had been spilled, the Duke's cavalry joined Giovanni's. An hour later, there was an explosion in the great square. It was the signal. All the church-bells began ringing violently; the markets suddenly closed; Giovanni's followers were increased by builders with hammers, butchers with cleavers, carpenters with stout poles and members of every craft, each with some instrument that could be used as a weapon. Gathering force like an angry fire, they

THE PAINTED DEATH

marched on the palace—foremost among them being Gian and the Deliverers.

And then a strange thing happened. The palace surrendered without a struggle. No soldiers appeared on the ramparts, not a missile was discharged through the narrow windows. As Gian and his band reached the walls, an old man with a scarred chin came out to greet him. It was Alessandro's court chamberlain and his favourite adviser.

" Enter, my lords," he said, with a mixture of civility and sarcasm. " It is a great day for deliverers."

Gian ignored the speech. " Where is your master ? " he asked.

" If you will follow me," said Alessandro's court chamberlain as though he were ushering them into a reception room, " I will show you."

" Wait a moment," whispered Lelio to Gian. " It sounds like a trap ! "

Gian turned to the advancing troops. " Some of you come with us ; some of you keep those doors open until the rest arrive."

They followed the old chamberlain through the portals. In the courtyard, huddled at the foot of the statue, lay a figure dressed in elaborate finery—like a life-size doll that had been smashed by being thrown from a great height.

" Alessandro ! " gasped Lelio. " Alessandro in his coronation clothes! But his face—" Lelio shuddered. " I always knew it was hateful. But this is horrible! It is scarcely a face at all!"

The court chamberlain pointed upward. " The tower," he said.

Giovanni's soldiers were filtering into the courtyard. They began to understand.

" This morning," the chamberlain continued in a feverishly tired voice, " this morning when the news of the uprising reached the palace, Duke Alessandro's own troops revolted. It was I who brought the news to the Duke. ' I shall speak to the mercenaries, myself,' he said and ordered the robes of state to be brought. The Duke's soldiers were conferring in the gallery when he found them. They gave him no opportunity to speak. Half a dozen of the cowards seized him from behind; another group swung him off his feet. They carried him to the top of the great tower. And—you see—"

The chamberlain pointed to the sprawled body and the unrecognisable face. The silks and velvets looked grotesque on that misshapen mass.

" Even the talisman of the Medici could not save him," said the chamberlain, lifting one of the bloodless hands. " You recognise the ring?"

" Yes," said Gian, " I recognise the ring."

At this moment the crowds broke in, flooding the courtyard. Yells of rage and triumph broke from them as they saw what

THE PAINTED DEATH

lay on the ground. They fell on the broken body, tearing its finery apart, hurling it from one to another as though it were a bundle of rotten rags. Neither Lelio nor Gian, who had already removed the ring, could stop them. Boxes were kicked in, the wood was piled up, straw put underneath and a torch set to the rubbish. Fifteen minutes later, the body—with what remained of the torn clothes—was tossed into the midst of the flames. Every member of the crowd had shreds of silk to keep as mementoes. Every one celebrated. The day was a long carouse ; the night was like day.

Even the Deliverers rejoiced, although with few words—all except Gian.

" I don't like it," he said, when the others questioned him. " There's something wrong."

" But," argued Prisco, " what can you expect of a mob ? I can't say that such a spectacle is very uplifting, but they've been waiting a long time. And a tyrant doesn't die every day."

" But is he dead ? " asked Gian. " It strikes me as queer."

" But, Gian," insisted Nanni, " you yourself saw Alessandro's body lying there—and you recognised the ring."

" I saw a body lying there," replied Gian. " And it is true that I recognised this ring. But I did not recognise the face." He paused a moment, and then went on as though he were thinking out loud. " Didn't it strike you," he said, " that there were several things peculiar about that body ? "

THE DONKEY OF GOD

" Peculiar ? " echoed Raffaelo. " In what way ? "

" Well," continued Gian, " first of all, is it usual for a ruler to put on coronation clothes merely to address his soldiers ? And then there were the hands. They were the hands of a peasant, not of an aristocrat. I have seen the hands of Alessandro and they were thin and smooth, not thick and spade-shaped like the ones we saw there. Then, as I removed the ring from the finger, I noticed a curious thing."

" Some distinguishing mark ? " interrupted Pandolfo.

" No mark at all," answered Gian. " And that is the more curious since it should have been there. After a ring is worn for some time, the friction and the pressure of the other fingers force it somewhat into the flesh. The flesh swells slightly around the ring, leaving a groove—whiter than the rest of the finger since the metal keeps off the sun—a groove which is not deep but deep enough to be noticed. When I removed the ring there wasn't a trace of a mark—the place where the groove should have been was as brown and thick as the rest of the finger."

" Which leads you to think—" Taddeo began.

" It leads me to believe," said Gian with a slight emphasis on the last word, " that the ring had never been on that finger before and that it was placed there only an hour or so before we arrived at the palace. The whole episode is queer, almost unreal. The court chamberlain, for instance—"

THE PAINTED DEATH

" But," said Taddeo, " his story was convincing and it fitted the accident."

" It fitted it entirely too well," said Gian. " Or perhaps it was the other way round; perhaps the accident fitted his story. I can't tell yet. But at the time I felt that the chamberlain was something of an actor—and now I begin to fear he's an actor in a very active sense. Think of it. Alessandro's chief adviser shows us a body so badly mutilated that no one can recognise a feature. Yet, though the face is a battered pulp, there is scarcely any blood on the fine silk and velvet cloak. That seems rather strange. Then, although there must have been many a blow exchanged—for Alessandro would not have let himself be murdered without a struggle—and though he was supposed to be thrown from a tower three hundred feet high, not a bone in his arm is broken. That's strange, too, isn't it? I particularly noticed that there wasn't the trace of a bruise on the wrist and forearm. It was that, more than anything else, which set me to wondering what had really happened."

This time there were no questions. The seven waited for the explanation which they knew was to come.

" What really happened, I imagine, was this," Gian resumed. " When Alessandro learned that Giovanni's soldiers would arrive here before the hired French troops, he knew he was lost—or would be, if he could not outwit his enemies.

THE DONKEY OF GOD

He knew the town had turned against him; he knew we were sworn to have his life; he knew he had no force to defeat us. If only he could gain time—if only he could deceive us until his bought troops arrived. He must have thought it all out the night before—probably he talked it over with the chamberlain—and in the morning, his plan was complete. Some one of the court attendants was conveniently killed. What was a murder more or less to Alessandro? Then the robes of state were put on the poor victim. Alessandro's mercenaries were sent out of the palace, and the Medici jewels carefully hidden—all except the talisman-signet which they placed on the finger that had never worn a ring before. After certain operations were performed on the poor corpse's face to make it unrecognisable, the body was placed dramatically in the centre of the courtyard, and the stage was set for the grand illusion. The chamberlain played his part beautifully, the scenery was perfect and the onlookers were thrilled. That, I believe, is how the farce was engineered. Meanwhile," continued Gian, " the chief actor is laughing at the success of his drama—not too boisterously, for it is unsafe to trust any walls in Florence—but laughing, nevertheless."

" Where? " exclaimed Prisco and Taddeo, voicing the thought of the others in one word and breath.

" Ah," said Gian. " That is one of the things for us to find out. The other thing we must discover is what our nimble

THE PAINTED DEATH

Alessandro has done with the Medici jewels—for, without these, he will not be able to bribe many armies. I suspect that where we find one we'll find the other." He smiled his peculiar smile again. " I had hoped to obtain some particulars from our friend, the chamberlain. But, after a few of the mildest methods of persuasion, the chamberlain succumbed to the rack and thumb-screws. I am afraid he had a bad heart, bad in more ways than one. But let us forget him. We must work in our own way—and we must not wait long."

Understanding was complete among them. They knew that Gian had uncovered one problem and was preparing to solve the next.

" How many days have we left ? " asked Lelio, speaking for them all.

" Four," answered Gian. " It ought to take five days for the French army to reach Florence ; six, if they meet bad weather. But we can't count on more than five. If they reach here before we have smoked our bird out of hiding, Florence will face another civil war, and the Deliverers will be known as the Despairers—if any of them are left. No, we must not lose a moment. Everything depends on the next and, I think, the final act of the drama."

" And when," asked Lelio, " do we begin ? "

" We have begun," answered Gian. " I have every reason to believe that Alessandro is still in the Palazzo Vecchio. Our men are searching it now. Let us all meet there one hour from now. In the same courtyard where the stage was set to fool us, we shall arrange another plot. Then we shall see what rôles we will have to play."

An hour later the eight gathered beneath the threatening tower now occupied by Giovanni's men. They had nothing to report. They had searched every room and corridor, but the entire palace was as empty as if it had never been occupied.

Gian looked doubtful but not disappointed.

"I scarcely expected to find him hiding in the main halls or playing puss-in-the-corner in the dining-room," he said. "This place is as full of half-concealed holes and chambers as a hollow tree. It will take all our attention for at least a day. A thorough search may reveal an unexpected passage in the most unlikely place."

But, at the day's end, the eight Deliverers confessed failure. Walls had been sounded for hollow spaces that might signify rooms; tapestries that could have hidden doors had been torn down; the wainscoting had been tapped for sliding panels; the chimney-places had been scoured for secret stairs; even the steps had been examined for trap-doors. But nothing had been found.

"Nothing," said Lelio, ruefully, "unless you call this something." He held up a torn shred of material for inspection.

"Where did you find it?" asked Gian.

THE PAINTED DEATH

" In the reception room, the room known as the Great Hall. It was hanging on a picture-frame."

Gian thought a moment.

" Can you remember which picture ? " he inquired.

" No," replied Lelio. " Does it matter ? "

" I'm afraid it does," said Gian. " And you couldn't say, could you, whether this piece was actually hanging from the frame or was caught on it, as if from some one brushing past ? No, I didn't think you could."

" What does the rag seem to be ? " Pandolfo asked in a careless gruffness that did not hide his curiosity.

" It is a part of a ribbon, a bright green ribbon," said Gian. " If I were fanciful, I would say it is snake-green, or poison-green, or a bright green that is, somehow, too bright. Since I am not indulging in fancies, I merely remark that this ribbon is of a kind and colour that I have not seen anywhere in Florence, nor, for that matter, on any dress or uniform in the palace at present."

" So you conclude—? " suggested Pandolfo.

" Nothing," answered Gian, his face relaxing from puzzled intensity to its usual puzzling smile. " It is too early for conclusions. But I will say that this torn ribbon strengthens my suspicion that our quarry is not far off. We must search still more thoroughly, and in more familiar quarters. But that will be to-morrow. There are just four nights and three days left."

THE DONKEY OF GOD

" And do we remain here ? " asked Prisco.

" Yes," answered Gian. " But not in a body. Our guards control the exits and entrances ; no one can leave or enter without our knowledge. There is no danger of attack. Yet there are several good reasons why we should separate for the night. You two, Pandolfo, and Neri, will occupy the painted room next to the terrace ; Prisco and Taddeo will take over the dining-room ; Nanni and Raffaelo will remain in the Great Hall ; while Lelio and I mount guard in the study."

It was a quiet household—quiet, said Lelio significantly, as the grave. Once Gian heard the soldiers changing guard and once he fancied he heard a scurrying of steps inside the wall. But it may have been a mouse, he reflected hopefully. And when Lelio woke at four in the morning—for they were sleeping in shifts—he turned over to dream of pictures draped in green ribbons that hid behind the wall.

At six they met in the courtyard. No one had noticed anything between midnight and dawn ; the night had been quite uneventful.

" But where," asked Lelio, " are Nanni and Raffaelo ? "

" Still sleeping, most likely," laughed Prisco. " Nanni said he hadn't slept in a week and Raffaelo probably found a goose-feather blanket. We'll find them snoring in the Great Hall."

" Let us hope so," said Gian. " But let us hurry."

Nothing stirred as they entered the Great Hall ; no one came

THE PAINTED DEATH

to greet them, least of all Nanni and Raffaelo. The two men appeared to be sleeping a few feet apart from each other, but it was too silent a sleep to promise anything but harm.

" Dead ? " whispered Lelio in a question that was its own answer. No one replied ; no reply was needed. Neri had lifted Nanni's arm, an arm that was cold and lifeless. Gian was already opening the neck of Raffaelo's shirt.

" No blood," he said, disrobing the body as quietly and coolly as though he were a doctor at an inquest. " No blows that I can see. Not a wound of any kind. No suspicion of violence. Let us examine Nanni. The same story. Nothing that can be seen. Yet here are two men—two of our dear friends—dead at our feet. But how ? "

" Alessandro," breathed Lelio, between hate and horror.

" Alessandro, of course," agreed Gian. " But how ? And with what ? Let us look closer."

But the most careful searching failed to disclose any evidence that might throw any light on the way the two Deliverers had met their death. Everything was as they had found it the night before. The windows, locked from the inside, were still tightly shut ; the floor showed no sign of having been disturbed ; the ceiling did not admit a hole large enough for a fly to crawl through. Gian then called the captain of the guard.

" You were on duty all last night ? " he asked.

"Ever since you retired and until you came down this morning," replied the captain.

"Did any one—even any of our own men—enter the Great Hall during the night?"

"No one."

"Are you sure?"

"Wait a moment." The captain wrinkled his dark forehead. "Yes, Andrea, one of my soldiers, was in the room for a minute or two."

"When was that?" asked Gian. "And how did he happen to be there?"

"It was shortly after midnight," answered the captain, speaking slowly. "Nanni called me and said he couldn't sleep; his throat was dry and the water wasn't fit to drink. I sent Andrea for a pitcher of wine and he fetched it here."

"Did you happen to taste it?"

"Well, yes," said the captain, reddening. "I did. I, too, was a bit thirsty—and—"

"Quite right, captain," said Gian. "I wanted to be sure that some one had. Did you notice anything queer about the wine—or about Andrea?"

"Not a thing," replied the captain promptly. "The wine was sweet—the new wine from Pistoia it was—and I must have swallowed a good goblet-full. As for Andrea, I'd vouch for the lad with my life."

THE PAINTED DEATH

"Well," interrupted Lelio, "since the captain had a gobletful with no ill results, the wine couldn't have been poisoned."

"Not," added Gian, " when Andrea brought it. But supposing that some one entered the room after Andrea and before Nanni and Raffaelo drank the rest of it—some one that had an object of getting rid of two powerful enemies without leaving a trace—such a person might well have added one of the quick and deadly drugs. It is hard to imagine such a possibility. The guards would have been sure to see the intruders. Nor is it easy to believe that Raffaelo and Nanni—granting they were awake—stood by silently while some one tampered with the pitcher, and then, after he had gone, calmly drank up the poisoned brew. Before we make any wild guesses, let us have a look at that wine-jug. We may learn something from the pitcher itself."

But the pitcher was not to be found. Prisco discovered a mark in the wood—a moist ring—which showed where it had been standing, but nothing else.

"It looks like ghosts' work," said Prisco.

"Or the work of a criminal," added Gian. "A clever criminal anxious to conceal every trace of his crime. He has overlooked nothing, while we are neglecting—something at least; perhaps several things. There are clues all about us, if we only knew where to find them. That bit of ribbon, for instance— it fits somewhere. Lelio found it on a picture-frame. Obviously, it doesn't fit there—people do not drape their paintings with gaudy green silk. But it is one clue which may lead to another. Meanwhile, let us examine the pictures."

They learned nothing there. The pictures were the usual assortment found in all medieval palaces: mythological subjects, allegories of the four seasons and the four elements, scenes from lives of various saints, and a host of portraits, mostly of the Medici family. The walls on which they were hung seemed solid; there was neither break nor crack in the plaster surface. It was dark before they finished—in fact they had to work quickly before evening set in and the flickering lamps made a shadowy uncertainty.

"One day gone—and two of our best men," said Pandolfo. "I don't suppose we can even give them a proper funeral."

"No," said Gian. "We must keep this set-back to ourselves. The captain will attend to the burial. We must prepare for tomorrow and keep a closer watch to-night. The terrace-room is too far-off for quick communication. We must occupy adjacent rooms. This time Lelio and I shall take up quarters in the Great Hall—"

"We cannot allow it," interposed Pandolfo. "Not when so much depends upon the next few hours. Either let me stay in the Great Hall or let us draw lots for the rooms."

The others seconded Pandolfo's objection; Gian saw it was best to yield. Slips of paper were prepared and shuffled. After

THE PAINTED DEATH

they had been drawn, it was decided that Taddeo and Pandolfo should watch in the Great Hall, Prisco and Neri in the study, with Leio and Gian in the adjacent dining-room. Unwilling to admit a sense of overhanging evil, they remained together long past midnight, alert for the lightest sound. It was three in the morning when they separated.

Weary though they were, neither Leio nor Gian could sleep. Every nerve was stretched, every vein tingled. Their very ears, as Lelio said later, stood on tiptoe. But no breath except their own stirred; the scurrying, of the mice—if mice they were— could not be heard here. At five, Gian opened the shutters on a grey dawn and a group of soldiers leaning on their arms. Half an hour later he said to Lelio, "Let us go downstairs— now."

Lelio rose without hesitation. "Did you hear anything?" he asked.

"No," replied Gian. "But I am worried. We have heard nothing and seen nothing—and I rather wish we had. This

fighting with a shadow is bad for the nerves; it's like stabbing the wind. I'll feel better after we've talked with the others."

Before reaching the corridor, they were joined by Prisco and Neri. But there was no response from the Great Hall.

"Pray God we're not too late," cried Gian and flung open the doors. The sight that greeted them was stupefying. Pan.

dolfo and Taddeo lay unmoving, stark, in a pool of blood At Gian's cry the captain of the guard ran in with six of his men.

"I'll swear that no one entered here—no one!" he exclaimed. "I stood just outside the doors with these very men A mouse couldn't have passed without our noticing it." The others stared, bewildered, speechless.

"And you heard nothing?" Gian asked with little hope.

"Nothing—neither from within the room nor outside."

"And yet," mused Lelio in a horrified voice," yet there they lie with their throats cut."

"Yes," whispered Gian. · And that makes it more than horrible. It makes it unbelievable. Look! Pandolfo's and Taddeo's swords are still in their scabbards; they have never beer drawn. Their bodies are cold, so it must have happened immediately after we left them. Yet no one entered these doors There was no outcry, no struggle. That is the unbelievable thing. Can you imagine the passionate Taddeo not drawing his sword at the first sign of danger? Can you picture our burly Pandolfo allowing his throat to be cut without a pro test? I said Alessandro was a clever criminal. I was wrong No criminal, no matter how clever, could accomplish this There's something devilish at work here. And, even if Alessandro should be the devil himself, we must stop the fiend's labours. If we fail again," Gian made an abrupt gesture, "we

THE PAINTED DEATH

are all dead men—and Florence, seized by mercenaries, will be a dead city."

He bent over Pandolfo and then Taddeo, examining the faces with great care.

"There's something about the mouth and nostrils that makes me think they were choked to death. But there are no marks upon the throat—and Pandolfo would have fought off any one who tried such tactics. Wait! Here are a few grains of something near the nostril."

He tried to gather them; but as he picked them up, they dissolved, leaving a pungent odour on the air.

"You recognise the smell?" inquired Gian of the others.

"No," answered Prisco. "But I noticed it as I stood near the corner of the further wall."

"Which corner?"

"This one, next to the large painting."

They searched the spot on hands and knees and were rewarded with an undissolved grain or two.

"I should have guessed it from yesterday's tragedy. Poison, of course. Somehow or other—and we must discover exactly how—poison has twice been spirited into this carefully guarded room. Raffaelo and Nanni were put out of Alessandro's way with a fatal drug added to the wine. Last night, since the watchers were on their guard against drinking, the method was changed although the means were the same. Poi-

THE DONKEY OF GOD

sons, or the fumes of poison, were introduced into this room until Pandolfo and Taddeo succumbed. Then, when they were unconscious, the fiend entered somehow, in some shape or other, and two more of his most dangerous enemies were easily disposed of. To-night—" He left the sentence open. There was no mistaking the sinister significance.

All day long they worked and far into the night with lamps, with magnifying water-glasses and all the candles they could command. At one o'clock the following morning, the searchers stopped. Nothing new had been learned.

"We could scarcely expect more," said Gian, as he dismissed the soldiers and the remaining four Deliverers sat in the Great Hall with their chins in their hands. "I am disappointed, yes; but not disheartened. I have a feeling that to-night will be the last night. The drama is about to end. Alessandro, with his jewels safe, with means to buy up the approaching army—and with two successful attacks on his enemies—will not fail to strike another blow. That will be our moment. We have much to avenge. I am curious to see what form that vengeance will take. But I confess I am equally curious to see what shape Alessandro assumes and by what agency he enters."

"And how shall the four of us divide?" asked Lelio.

"To-night we remain together," said Gian. "It will need the combined vigilance of all of us. I have already instructed

THE PAINTED DEATH

the captain to post his men not only at every gate and doorway, but under every window, even though the lowest windows are twenty feet above the ground. At the first hint of disturbance in this room, his soldiers will be here, ready for anything. Meanwhile, I suggest that the four of us settle ourselves near the four corners of this place to watch—this time with drawn swords!"

"And if anything appears—" began Prisco.

"No matter what shape it may wear, strike—strike and shout!" said Gian. Then he added grimly, "He may get one of us before we get him, but even the devil cannot be in four different corners at the same time."

The ordeal of waiting began. Fagged though they were, no one closed an eye. By Gian's orders, no one spoke; the four did not even exchange whispers. Secrecy, said Gian, must be fought with secrecy. An hour passed in utter silence. Two hours. Three. Toward morning a light scuffling sound in the wall began; but, after a few minutes, the mouse-like scurrying ceased. Silence—a long blank stillness—set in.

If a mouse moved, it moved quieter than the hours.

The air in the room grew heavier. It was a sweet heaviness. A candle went out. Another. After two sleepless nights, the fragrant silence was a comfort. Gian breathed more deeply. His head nodded; his chin sank on his breast.

Gian started up suddenly. A wind was in the closed room:

THE DONKEY OF GOD

it had blown the candles out. At the same moment he heard a shout, " The picture ! The picture ! "

Seizing his lamp, Gian rushed to the opposite corner. It was Prisco, bleeding from half a dozen wounds. " The picture ! " he gasped. " The painted death ! Look ! " Prisco held up one hand, trying to point with a great effort. " He came—too quick for me ! " And Prisco fainted. But not before Gian noted a torn bit of green silk in the closed fingers.

By this time the guards were in the Great Hall. Torches showed that Prisco's injuries were not fatal. Leaving the captain to attend to the wounded man, Gian held his lamp close to the wall, scanning the paintings. It was the corner they had examined hastily at the end of the previous day. Gian noticed nothing unusual, either in the designs of the first two pictures or the way in which they were framed. But the face of the third held him from going further; in the flickering light it almost leaped from its canvas. It was the face of a youth between boyhood and manhood. The lips curved curiously above a child-like chin; the deep-set eyes were dark with contradictions; the forehead was unwrinkled ivory. And yet there was something sinister about the face; something that was not in any one feature, but lay, rather, behind them all. The very innocent expression of the mouth made the sense of evil the more terrible, as though a child had been learned in the ways of a fiend. Even as he looked at it, Gian felt ill.

THE PAINTED DEATH

Then Gian suddenly realised that the feeling of faintness had a more physical cause. The light of his lamp was reflected by a ring on the hand of this painting—a ring that was not painted but made of metal so thin that it lay flat on the canvas. And, at the same moment that Gian noticed this strange thing, he was aware of a breath coming out of it. It was a vapour, an invisible powdery puff of air. As Gian bent nearer, his knees sagged; he reeled and had to hold fast to the picture to keep from falling. As he swayed, he fancied the frame swayed too.

" Neri ! Lelio ! " he shouted. " The frame ! It gives ! " But though the three friends strained their utmost, they could do nothing ; it would not budge.

" Fool that I was ! " cried Gian. " It is the picture, not the frame. The secret is in the ring ! "

He dug at the thin bit of metal with his knife, pierced it and pried it loose. As he did so, the end of a tube fell through the canvas and a cloud of poisonous fumes arose as the painting swung back within the wall. The astonished three could see nothing but a black hole, an opening half the size of a man, until Gian, holding a handkerchief over his mouth and nostrils, plunged his lamp in the opening. The light revealed a flight of narrow stairs.

" Don't breathe for a moment ! " cried Gian. " Shield your faces and follow me ! "

They had not long to climb. Nor did they fail to find what

THE DONKEY OF GOD

they were seeking. Within a few seconds they stumbled into a small, evil-smelling room. And there, surrounded by potions and death-dealing powders, as well as the Medici jewels, crouched Alessandro. In his suit of harsh green silk, he seemed more poisonous than the poisons he brewed.

" At last ! " cried Gian, seizing the tyrant and sending Alessandro's dagger to the floor.

But Lelio interposed. " No ! No ! " he begged.

" What ! " exclaimed Gian. " You want me to spare him ? "

" Only that I may have the pleasure of despatching him, myself. I was not always called Lelio. I was christened Lorenzino, the little Lorenzo, after my famous grandfather. And I have much to revenge besides the murder of my brother, Ippolito. I have taken an oath to do it ! "

" Confidence for confidence," said Gian. " I was not always called Gian. In fact, until the Deliverers were organised, I was known as Giovanni. I am still called that by my troops : Giovanni the Freebooter, or Giovanni of the Black Band."

" The curse of hell upon you ! " screamed Alessandro. It was the first sentence he had uttered in their presence. It was also the last. Gian stood aside while Lelio—or Lorenzino—fulfilled his vow. Florence was avenged. And so were the four dead companions.

A day later, when the French troops reached the gates of Florence, they received a rude shock. Instead of Alessandro's

THE PAINTED DEATH

envoys laden with jewels and other bribes, they were met by Giovanni's black-banded soldiers. The disappointed mercenaries hesitated; they then departed, attending quickly to their own affairs.

So Florence was not merely avenged; she was saved. And her saviour was Giovanni, or, as they continued to call him the rest of his life, Gian the Deliverer.

Thus the fiction. The facts, as they are recorded in more trustworthy if drier history, are as follows:

Alessandro, surnamed "the Moor," was actually the most hated despot Florence ever endured. He had been created Duke in 1532 and kept power by the aid of Charles V, the French king, one of whose daughters he had married. He got rid of most of his rivals—chiefly by poisoning them—among his victims being the Cardinal Ippolito. Four years later (in 1536) he was assassinated by his own cousin Lorenzino. Immediately after his death, he was followed by Giovanni Bande Nere, a soldier of fortune, a descendant of the original Medici family and a man of extraordinary bravery as well as "the greatest commander produced by Italy in the Sixteenth Century." Giovanni's son became the founder of the junior branch of the Medici, Cosimo I, who reigned almost forty years and combined the various territories of Florence into one great state.

Nothing more was heard of the Deliverers. They were no longer needed.

VENICE

VENICE

VENICE

VENICE is one of the most peculiar as well as one of the most picturesque cities in the world. It is not merely an island, it is one hundred and seventeen islands. Though none of these is of any great size, there are enough of them to require some four hundred bridges, most of the bridges being made of ancient stone. There are no motors, no horses, no trolleys, no buses in Venice, for the excellent reason that there are no streets. Instead of pavements and promenades, there are avenues and alleys made of water, there being no less than one hundred and fifty of these water-ways or canals.

Thus Venice is not only built in the midst of water, but actually on it. The tide rises against the very steps of the buildings, slaps against the walls, and gives one the impression of a magician's pleasure-city floating upon the sea. To be more realistic, although Venice, like Venus, rose from the water, she does not float upon it; she rests very solidly on her unstable-looking foundation. The marble domes, the fluted balconies, the lordly columns, the carved arcades rest securely

THE DONKEY OF GOD

on supports of wood and stone; it is said that more than a million piles uphold this island empire situated on the coast of Italy half-way between Florence and fairyland.

Lacking motors, cabs and cars, we must get on without them. Yet, rather than swim, we look for some means of conveyance. We look, hoping to find, in so fantastic a place, something wild and strange, something out of the Arabian Nights. We are not disappointed. Here the gondola, that strange bark, is at home. The gondola looks like a long dark bird with a huge, sharp-cutting beak—a cross between a black swan and a water-serpent. Weird, gliding creatures they are and weird cries come from them, especially at night.

But it does not take you long to discover that appearances are deceptive, especially in Venice, that this queer craft is the Venetian's taxi, and that the peculiar bird-like cries are made by the boatmen. It is something of a jar for the poetic nature when it realises that the melancholy chant "Ah-oh-el!" signifies "Look out!" and that the tune of a romantic despair means nothing more than "Keep to the right." Every gondolier is supposed to be another Caruso, just as every Italian child is supposed to sing Verdi in his cradle. But most of the operatic boatmen who misguided me past the museums I wanted to see into the lace-factories I did not want to visit, seemed to be suffering from too much energy and enlarged tonsils.

VENICE

Nevertheless, the gondolier is extraordinarily skilled—only the most sensitive oarsman could guide so large a craft through thread-like canyons and around razor-edged corners—and most people still prefer the little covered cabins of the gondola to the larger and more recent motor-boats. Whatever he may lack as a tenor, the gondolier is a model of dexterity and grace. Balanced by the iron beak or prow, he stands on the raised rear end, known as the "poppa," scarcely moving. His paddle, which is more like a pole, barely ripples the water; his body shows not the slightest sense of effort. Yet the long boat swerves on its own axis, turns tail, thrusts itself ahead, or glides to your destination with an ease that is like no motion you have ever felt except in dreams.

There are two Venices, the Venice of the nonchalant native and the Venice of the astonished sight-seer. Both meet, morning, noon and night, in the great Piazza of Saint Mark. Here the word "great," too large for most things it usually accompanies, is too small. Applied to this glory of a square, "great" becomes meagre, miserable, minus. To describe this plaza one needs new gigantic words, words that have never been used to advertise soups or cigarettes or super-cinemas, words that exist only on some furthest, undiscovered star and would be written in letters of light.

Lacking such words, let it be prosily stated that the first sight of the Piazza of Saint Mark is so dazzling that the eye

THE DONKEY OF GOD

cannot rest on any one spot. In front of you (if you enter it the " right " way) rises the magnificent San Marco, or the Church of Saint Mark, enshrining the bones of the Evangelist. On each side are palaces of the highest officials of the ancient Venetian Republic, as well as the Old Library (" perhaps the most magnificent secular edifice in Italy "), founded by the poet Petrarch who, settling in Venice, made the city a gift of his valuable collections. In one corner built on top of a gateway is the curious clock-tower and its bronze giants. In another corner is the Piazzetta, or Little Piazza, with its square campanile (bell-tower) and the much-pictured granite columns—one bearing a statue of Saint Theodore, the other supporting the winged Lion of Saint Mark, the Gospel held in his right paw. The Piazzetta is half-enclosed by the splendid Palace of the Doges (or Dukes) and ends abruptly with a brilliantly reflecting sea which makes the marbles seem even more dazzling than they are.

The winged lion is everywhere in Venice. Sometimes he crouches; sometimes he stands up fiercely; sometimes his strength seems to be in the Book he leans on; sometimes he brandishes a sword. But he is always in sight. And naturally so. Every Italian town had its figure that served as emblem, mascot and device—a protection as well as a proclamation. Florence flaunted the patrician lily. Perugia displayed the griffon—or, as readers of " Alice in Wonderland " may prefer,

VENICE

the gryphon—on her shield. The men of Pisa always carried their eagle with them when they went to war and his screams were supposed to bring fear to the enemy and triumph to the Pisans. The winged lion was, however, the most powerful of all the emblems for, so the Venetians contended, he came straight out of the Bible, being the pet beast of one of the four Evangelists, and the greatest of these.

There is less authority for the tale of the two bronze giants on the clock-tower, but it is a rare story.

In the days when wonders happened more frequently than not and strange adventures were a small part of the day's work, there lived two giants who had become much talked about. The rest of their tribe had died out and their nearest relatives, who had gone to live in the caves of the far North, were quiet and God-fearing creatures. But these two, whose names happened to be Ferro and Forte, respected nothing and no one. They laboured morning and afternoon, night after night, sleeping only one day every twelve months—and that day being the shortest day of the year. Mining was their work; digging metal their pleasure. So greedy were they to collect all the iron and copper in Italy that they tore down hills, uprooted forests and wrecked mountain-pastures in their haste. Nor was that the worst. So noisy were they at their labours—for they had voices that matched their size—that no one for miles around could sleep. Heroes had been advertised for; large rewards for giant-killers had been posted in all the villages near Venice. But no rescuer appeared, and the country-folk had nothing to fall back on except their prayers.

Yet when things are at their worst and hope is feeblest, nothing is more powerful than prayer. One day—it happened to be a Sunday—an Angel of the Lord appeared to the two giants. Ferro had just finished throwing down ten wagon-loads of iron with a deafening clatter and Forte was picking it up with an even louder noise.

"Where are you going?" said the Angel of the Lord.

"To Venice," replied Ferro, "if it's any of your business."

"It is my Lord's business," answered the Angel quietly.

"It is because of Him that I am here."

"Well," growled Forte, "what does He want? Don't keep us standing here!"

"He wants you to remember the Sabbath," said the Angel, more quietly than ever. "You must keep the Sabbath holy, On it you shall not labour nor do any work."

"The Sabbath?" asked Ferro, with a sneer. "That's the day when your Lord tires of working—once every seven days isn't it?"

VENICE

"There is a time for everything," quoted the Angel." There is a time to break down and a time to build up, a time to cast way and a time to gather together, a time for labour and a time to cease from—"

"That's all very fine," interrupted Forte," but we have better things to do than listen to a sermon. Besides, we're not interested in the Sabbath. It may be all right for the lazy men and women who worship your Lord, but not for us. We're too busy."

"And," added Ferro, "we don't care about time, either. We are above Time and his little hours. We will sing when we want to and dig where we please."

"And now," concluded Forte, "we go to attack the foundations of Venice—Sabbath or no Sabbath!"

"Very well," said the Angel, so quietly that the giants did not notice how grim he had become. "Very well. You shall go to Venice. And you shall never be parted from the copper and iron you dig without stopping; indeed, they shall be part of you. And you shall be above Time. Oh, yes, you shall be above it. But you shall obey it. Of a surety, you shall not forget Time and his little hours.' Oho! You shall keep account of time 's smallest divisions. Yes, you shall keep a count of them forever. You shall watch the tiny minutes crawl like iron tortoises and even the winged seconds will seem like bronze eternities to you."

THE DONKEY OF GOD

And there on the clock-tower, they stand to-day, those two giants, changed into the metal they loved too well. They are " above Time " in one sense at least, for the platform on which they stand is a hundred feet above the blue and gold dial which records the minutes. But they are not too far above Time to forget to obey it. On the contrary. They wait, those two giants, until the despised minutes crawl around like iron tortoises, and then they are more bound to Time than ever. With their hammers of iron and copper they must labour, striking the bell between them, announcing the hours of their servitude. Thus Ferro, the iron one, and Forte, the strong one, have become the slaves of Venice as well as the servants of God. And on the Sabbath they strike the hours of rest with a special sound, a chime which adds the thanksgiving of rest to the song of labour.

Saint Mark is the patron saint of Venice—the church at the head of the Piazza being the most elaborate of his monuments—yet he was not born in Venice nor did he ever live there. When the evangelist was preaching the Gospel, he travelled through Italy. From Rome he went to Rimini, and from there to the smaller towns along the Eastern coast. A storm drove him on one of the sand-banks where Venice is now situ-

VENICE

ated and, since there was not the slightest sign of shelter, the saint gave himself up for lost. As he knelt down for his last prayer, the sky cracked and out of the lightning stepped an angel. " Peace to thee, Mark," cried the heavenly messenger. " This is not the end of thy labours, but the beginning. Thou shalt travel far and ever further; thou shalt not die until thou art revered by the greatest city. Yet, though thou shalt be buried as Bishop of Alexandria, thy bones shall find their resting-place on this shoal in the heart of this uninhabited lagoon."

The prophecy was fulfilled, though it took almost a thousand years. When Attila the Hun ran fire and sword through Italy, the towns near the lagoon were laid waste. Those who could escape fled to the network of islands where the channels were so few and the sand-banks so treacherous that the homeless ones were not pursued. " Cut off from cities and supplies, they will die of fever and starvation," thought their enemies. But those who were once citizens of wealthy towns learned a new and simpler way of life; they taught themselves to fish, to make boats, to navigate the most dangerous harbours. Soon the first church was erected, strengthened with marble from the ruins on the mainland; soon they had made a city and a civilisation. From a possibility the Venetian navy became a power. Then one day, in the year 829, a Venetian ship brought the body of St. Mark from Alexandria to the

THE DONKEY OF GOD

new church which was being built on the very sand-bank where the evangelist had been stranded. No one knew how the sacred bones had been obtained, although foul play and bribery were suspected. But the prophecy had been fulfilled and, a few years later, Venice had a shrine as great as St. Peter's in Rome. By the end of the Tenth Century the church of St. Mark's was one of the world's wonders. Every ship that came to Venice brought treasures for its enrichment: alabaster and curiously veined marbles, odorous woods for the mosaics, gold and jewels for the *pala d'oro*, that superb piece of Byzantine jeweller's work which crowns the high altar. The evangelist's lion was seen everywhere; his image guarded home and harbour; the angel's greeting, " Pax tibi, Marce " (" Peace to thee, Mark "), became the state motto.

The church remains worthy of its saint. Time has not cheapened its proportions nor dulled its colours. The effect, with its many mounting domes and five hundred marble columns, is delicate, fantastic and monstrous with the richness of the East. It seems to have grown like the Oriental stories which inspired it.

The palace of the Doges is as old and almost as exquisite as its neighbour, St. Mark's. Here all the styles meet without prejudice—Oriental, Gothic, Renaissance—none takes command, none contradicts the other. It is hard to decide whether to look longer at the rich upper arcade known as *La Loggia*,

VENICE

like lace in stone; or the statues of Adam and Eve; or spend most time in the interior with its succession of princely rooms acting as a sumptuous background for the paintings of Tintoretto, Palma Giovane and, particularly, Paolo Veronese. Here is the overpowering " Paradise," Tintoretto's masterpiece, the world's largest painting with more than five hundred figures, and here are some of the most sumptuous ceilings eyes have strained to see. Here the Great Council sat to determine the conduct of the state; here the all-powerful Ten issued orders which were to " hold the gorgeous East in fee "; here plots were hatched which poets and dramatists have seized on. Only the Academy of Fine Arts, with its Bellinis and Titians, offers a grander display of pictures; only the Grand Canal is more truly Venetian.

If you can imagine a combination of business street, a double row of palaces, a ghetto and the Arabian Nights—and then place the result in the midst of water, you will have something like the Grand Canal. Herr Baedeker, at the mention of whose name all good travellers cross themselves, describes it as " this magnificent thoroughfare, one of the finest in the world," adding that it is adorned with about two hundred palaces, mostly dating from the Fourteenth to Eighteenth Centuries and every bend in its S-shape course reveals new beauties. Description is useless—even Herr Baedeker, for all his astounding information, does not dare attempt it. You will understand why as soon as you make your first trip down this chief artery of traffic. Take a gondola—the motor-launches move too quickly—and take your time, for every foot of the two miles is crowded with romantic beauty and rich associations. Here—and guides, gondoliers and gratis charts will tell you precisely where—are the buildings which endear Venice to every visitor: the ornately rounded church of Santa Maria della Salute; the house which legend has assigned to Desdemona; the palazzo bearing a memorial tablet which tells of Robert Browning's death there in 1889; the triple palace of Mocenigo occupied by Byron in 1818; the Palazzo Loredan, dating from the Twelfth Century, which Ruskin declared was the least conspicuous but most beautiful in the whole extent of the Canal; the building—one of the most attractive in Venice—where the composer Richard Wagner died. Here, connecting the east and west quarters of the town, is the bridge of the Rialto, flanked by shops—a district remembered by all who remember Shylock—and here is the *Ca' d'Oro*, the famous "Golden House" whose gilded arches and pillars could be seen, they say, even through the darkest nights.

As the schoolboy put it, "At every part of the Grand Canal, one stands with open mouth, drinking it all in."

The principal "sights" of Venice can be "seen" in three days. Closer study and more intimate details could keep you for as many months—or years. There is Lido (literally "sand-

VENICE

bank "), the last word in bathing-beaches, where you can scarcely see the water because of the celebrities. There are the three near-by islands which can be visited in one day: Murano, where the delicate Venetian glassware has been made ever since 1290, and where you can see copies of the antique vases being blown to-day; Burano, home of the costly point-lace (*point de Venise*) and an interesting fishing-village; Torcello, that solitary shrouded isle with its cathedral dating from the early Ninth Century, and its Byzantine mosaics. There is the day's trip to Padua, celebrated as the place where St. Anthony was born and Giotto painted his finest frescoes.

But everything brings you back to the square of St. Mark's where the four bronze horses are just as much at home in the central arch of a Christian church as on the pagan arch of Nero, their first eminence. Nor will you forget the pigeons of the Piazza. In fact, you cannot forget them. They are as populous, as persistent and ever-present as the pigeons of St. Paul's in London, and rare is the visitor who escapes without being photographed feeding them. The commerce and conquest of the Venetian Republic has dwindled to tourists with visas in one hand and a bag of corn in the other. Yet, in spite of her fall from glory, though her islands are plural and plebeian, Venice is still " the city noble and singular."

DAUGHTER OF THE LION

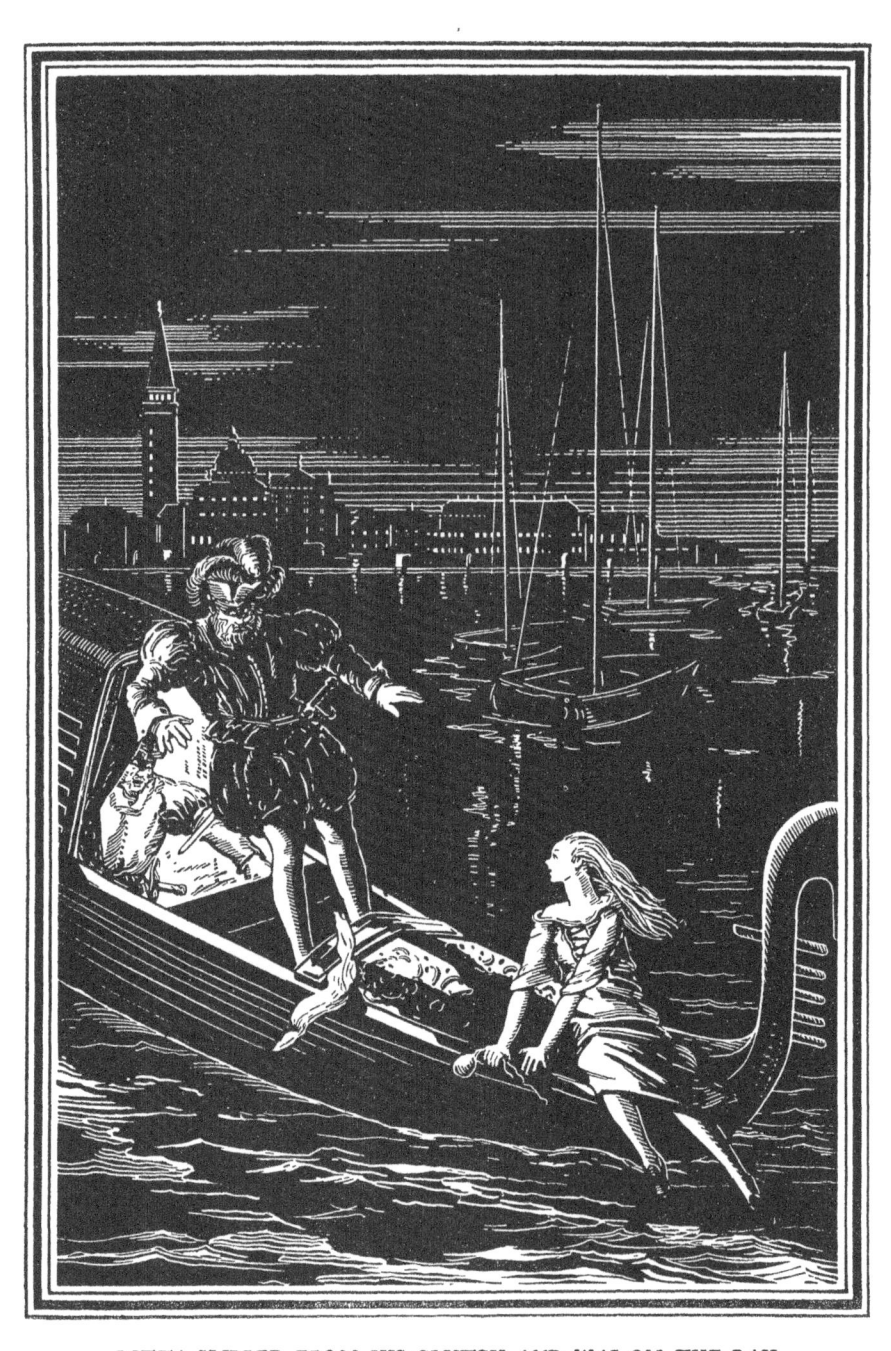

DITTA SLIPPED FROM HIS CLUTCH AND WAS ON THE RAIL

DAUGHTER OF THE LION

THE *Bucintoro*, that magnificent galley, floated majestically down the Grand Canal. Never had a barge of state shone with such splendour. Every foot of it sparkled with a hundred colours. Eighteen artists had worked for a year painting the history of Venice around its upper deck, modelling the figurehead, carving and gilding its sides and balconies. The decks were inlaid with ebony and mother-of-pearl; fluted pillars supported a canopy of brocaded velvet and gold; the eighty-six oars had been silvered, and one hundred and seventy-two rowers manned the royal craft. No wonder Venice was packed to its last crowded inch with visitors from the neighbouring islands, from the mainland, even from foreign provinces. The lightest breeze could not wedge itself among the throngs on the Piazza, and the water was black with boats.

For Venice was celebrating three events in one: Ascension Day, the election of the new Doge, and the arrival of the Ambassador from England. The first of these marked the begin-

THE DONKEY OF GOD

ning of a four days' festival and it was awaited the more eagerly because it started with the picturesque *Sposalizio del Mare*, " The Wedding of the Sea." Next to St. Mark, the sea was Venice's greatest protection : it brought her tribute from the furthest corners of earth ; it built natural barriers for miles about her ; it made devious channels that no enemy could navigate. Therefore, every Ascension Day, the Doge, as head of the state, acted as priest and married Venice to the waters.

The *Bucintoro* made for the open sea, followed by gondolas and barges of every description. Patricians and shopkeepers, princes and vagabonds in anything that would float saw the Doge stand with a commanding gesture. About him were the Senators, the Great Council and the embassies from France, Spain and England. They too rose as a trumpet spoke and the Doge extended his hand. Silence fell suddenly ; even the waves ceased their loud sliding and slapping as the Doge said, " O Sea, in the name of Venice, we take thee to wife. Thou who hast proved watchful in the past, be faithful now. With this ring we espouse thee—blessed be the union." And, in token of consent, he dropped the nuptial ring into the bosom of the Adriatic. Then the bands broke into festive marches ; the people cheered ; the church-bells rang their loudest wedding-peals.

Ditta hugged herself with pleasure. (She had been christened Editta, but no one had time to call her that.) It was her great festival ; it was Holy Thursday ; she was fifteen. She

DAUGHTER OF THE LION

lived with her Aunt Emmi and Uncle Nicolo in one of the oldest corners of the Rialto. The family was not so poor as to be in need, not so rich as to afford idle nieces. So Ditta worked, helping her cousins market the fish which her uncle caught. A tall, slender girl she was with a fine head, though far from beautiful. But three things set her apart from the other girls in the neighbourhood: her yellow hair, her cornflower-blue eyes, and her unusual strength. " Why," said her Uncle Nicolo when, on her tenth birthday, she downed the largest of her boy-cousins and sat on him triumphantly, " she isn't a girl-child, she's a young army. She's a true daughter of the lion ! "

The name clung to her and Ditta grew to accept it, even to cherish it. Never having seen her father, who died before she was born, Ditta almost claimed kinship with the king of beasts. Whenever she passed the unprotected standing lion on St. Mark's or the sitting one in front of the Arsenal, she would whisper, " And how is my noble father to-day ? " And the stone monument would reply—though none but Ditta could hear him—" Fairly, Ditta, only fairly. The fog has been getting in my throat and there are too many pigeons nowadays." " Stupid birds ! " Ditta would scold as she brushed the too-familiar creatures away. " They never learn their place ! " " Thank you, my daughter," the lion would say to her. " Be blessed. And be worthy of your father." Then it would become a silent stone again and Ditta would know the conversation was over.

THE DONKEY OF GOD

Her talks with the marble beast were never long. But they gave Ditta new strength and she would put her shoulder to the wheel or ply the gondola or lift the heavy baskets with more ease than ever. Every night she would help with the sorting, and every morning she would hold up the catch and cry, " Fine fresh fish ! Who'll buy ? Fat red mullet ! Silver shiners ! Sweet turbot ! Fine fresh fish to-day ! Who'll buy ? " Every day brought more work and every day she accomplished it without complaint, almost without effort.

But to-day was holiday. No one in the crowd on the Piazza had cheered louder than Ditta. To a fisherman's niece the marriage of Venice and the sea was more important than any wedding of human beings. Second to her lions, she loved her city. Ditta had never been happier than now. It was only when the crowd was breaking up that she grew troubled. There was nothing to disturb her—the city was celebrating in every key and colour, the music was gay, the sky foretold good fishing—nothing except a group of three men. In spite of all jostling, the three remained together.

" Absurd," she told herself, " even though one is a Venetian noble, one a common French sailor, and one wears an English doublet and hose. It's absurd to let that trouble me. And yet," she went on, still to herself, but also to St. Mark's lion a hundred feet above her, " what brings an ordinary French seaman and a Venetian noble together ? And why is that patrician here

DAUGHTER OF THE LION

in this crowd instead of following the *Bucintoro* in his gondola ? And where does the English gentleman fit in ? "

This was evidently too puzzling for the lion, for he did not utter a single syllable. But Ditta thought he pressed his stony lips together as if to say, " Whoever they are, they're up to no good. They'll bear watching. If I were you, I'd follow and keep my eye on them." " I will ! " said Ditta, and jumped to find she had said it out loud.

An hour later, Ditta was crouching outside of a wine-shop where the three men had entered. They had asked the innkeeper for a private room in the back, and Ditta, pretending to doze in the sunlight, listened underneath the lattices. It was a warm day and the wooden blinds were not quite closed. At first all she could hear was a confused murmur and gurgling ; but as the Chianti flowed faster the voices grew louder. The Venetian noble did most of the talking. Finally, he shrugged and threw up his hands.

" Very well," he said with a sour laugh. " You win. We Venetians are poor bargainers. You, my Lord Rosslyn—"

" Mr. Smith," interrupted the Englishman.

" To be sure, Mr. Smith," smiled the Venetian. " And you, Captain Villegrand—"

" Common Sailor Jacques Paul, *if* you please," murmured the Frenchman.

" Jacques Paul, of course. Pardon the slip of memory. You,

THE DONKEY OF GOD

Jacques Paul, promise to have your ship in readiness; and you, Mr. Smith, guarantee to deliver the young lady into my hands. I, on my part, will raise the reward to the amount specified. And when I am Doge, I will see to it that England and France have free entry and the favour of the State. Is that clear ? "

" Perfectly clear," said the French captain in sailor's costume. " Except that France does not become your ally until the paper is signed."

" You realise," grumbled the Venetian, " that my signature is my death-warrant—if this paper is ever discovered. Still—"

In the silence Ditta could hear the scratching of a quill-pen. " Is there anything else ? "

" Only this," said the English lord. " I did not guarantee to put my mistress actually into your hands. The young princess is so closely guarded that a public kidnapping would be impossible. I did promise to show you a way. And it is this : To-morrow night all Venice will celebrate high Carnival. The Piazza will be packed to see the water-illuminations and every one will be masked. I happen to know that the whim of the Princess is to mingle in the crowd near the pavilion and that, to disguise herself, she is going to wear the rags of a beggar. During the second intermission, after the fireworks are again under way, I shall create a diversion of some sort—start a quarrel or fall in a faint. That will be your time. You and your men will have their opportunity. You will have to work quickly. What you do after that will be equally difficult. But that is your own affair."

"What I will do after that is simple," said the Venetian. "I will have her gagged and brought in my own gondola to the French ship. And there, thanks to—er—Jacques Paul, the young lady will vanish from our story. The hue and cry will be prolonged—especially by the English Embassy. It will be most unpleasant for the present Doge; the more unpleasant since relations between England and Venice have been at the breaking-point. If the present Doge is careful of his neck, he will fly the country; if he is not, he will find himself descending the Golden Stairs of his palace for the last time— while I ascend them."

The suave Venetian voice paused for a moment. Then it went on a little more anxiously.

"But how am I to be sure of the lady? A sixteen-year-old princess masquerading as a beggar is apt to look like any other beggar of the same age—and there are more than a few of them in Venice."

"You will recognise her by several things," said the Englishman. "For one thing, she is taller than your Venetians; for another, she is blonde and blue-eyed. Besides that, she will be at the water-front close to the pavilion. And lastly, in spite

THE DONKEY OF GOD

of her rags, she will be wearing the bloodstone seal-ring of the royal house."

Taller than the Venetians; blonde, and blue-eyed; sixteen—"Why," thought Ditta, "except for the difference of a year and the royal ring, he might be describing me." Then as she heard the chairs scrape, she knew the conspirators had risen, and Ditta slid around the corner.

What to do, she thought, as she hurried toward the Rialto, whom should she tell? Should she go to the Grand Council and reveal all she had heard? But they would laugh at her, demand a proof, or, possibly, punish her for inventing so wild a tale. Besides, the Grand Council would never allow the niece of a fisherman in their august presence. The guards would stop her at the door and tell her that all accusations must be put in writing and dropped in the *Bocca di Leone*, the public complaint-box. The letter would then be read in a week or two. But after to-morrow night it would be too late. Besides, Ditta could not write.

"What to do," repeated Ditta under her breath, but loud enough to be heard by the lion in front of the Arsenal. "Whom to tell?"

"Tell no one, my daughter," she fancied her father's spirit replying. "Keep your own counsel—be your own Council."

"Yes," said Ditta to herself. "He is right. It is better that way. If I think hard, perhaps a plan may come. Is it not so?"

DAUGHTER OF THE LION

The lion said nothing, but a shadow passed over his forehead and the eyes closed in agreement. He was right. That evening Ditta was back with a scheme worked out to the last detail. The lion never once interrupted her as she explained what she proposed to do, and at the end she stood up in excitement.

"So," whispered Ditta, "I shall save the Princess. And I shall save Venice. But you must help. If you disapprove of my plan, tell me and I will act as you say. All you need do is shake your head or mutter 'No!'"

But the lion neither muttered nor shook his head, and Ditta knew she was to go on with her counter-plot. It was a daring scheme and a dangerous one; it required all her strength and a swiftness such as she had never needed. But when Ditta woke the next morning everything was clear and she was confident.

Only two people shared her secret: her Aunt Emmi and her Uncle Nicolo. It seems strange that they should have followed Ditta's lead, but Uncle Nicolo had always trusted Ditta more than he could trust his eldest son, and a fortune-teller had told Aunt Emmi that honour would be brought to the family by one outside it.

"Don't worry, either of you," cried Ditta, as she left them, stuffing an extra bit of *torrone* in the square of cotton which was both cap and kerchief. "Have my bed made up with the

THE DONKEY OF GOD

Christmas covers, Aunt Emmi. And, Uncle Nicolo, don't forget the boat-pillows. And be sure to have the gondola closer to the Piazza steps than any of the others."

She vanished to have a last word with her fatherly lion.

At midnight the masquerade began. The streets had been thronged with merry-makers long before dark; at sunset the Doge had thrown doves to the people—an event that, heretofore, only happened on Palm Sunday—the Pope's emissary had scattered money among the poor, and the new angel of the bell-tower had been baptised in milk, sea-water and wine. There had been athletic sports and bull-baiting in the Piazza. A troupe of foreign acrobats had made a pyramid almost as high as St. Theodore's column, and a Turkish tight-rope walker had descended across the square to the feet of the Doge, while all Venice held its breath. At ten o'clock there had been a play of jugglers who kept a dozen lighted torches twirling in the air.

But it was not until midnight, with the first explosion of Roman candles, that the Carnival officially began. Other nations, ran the proverb, use their powder for war; the Venetians use theirs—when it is dry—for fireworks. The display had never been more brilliant than to-night. Rockets rose screaming from the barges and died in a shower of stars; a hundred fiery wheels burned across the sky, while the water, reflecting them, seemed madly ablaze; flowers of many-coloured flame blossomed out of each other, twisting and towering into new and monstrous shapes.

Before the first intermission, Ditta, her hair tied up in the handkerchief and her clothes more ragged than the poorest beggar, had wormed her way through the crowds. Now she stood close to the pavilion where the foreign ambassadors had been given the place of honour. Soon, unnoticed in the fitfully lit darkness, she stood next to the English princess.

"*Principessa*," began Ditta. "*Permesso*—"

But the Princess understood no Italian. Ditta, who knew no English, had not thought of this emergency. It looked as if all her plans would fall because of this one small stumbling-block. Suddenly Ditta remembered there was an older language than speech. With a mysterious gesture and a very real secrecy, Ditta plucked the torn sleeve of the royal masquerader and jerked a thumb seaward. The Princess shook a puzzled head, but she was curious. The night had given her her first taste of liberty—costume and mask had freed her from tiresome court etiquette—and this ragged girl, about her own height, promised adventure. Ditta pointed one arm at the sky, the other toward the bridge of boats. The Princess began to understand. To see the fireworks from the water— from a gondola, with a companion her own age instead of a lot of stupid chamberlains and stiff ladies-in-waiting—what a lark! She followed Ditta.

It was only a few steps to the landing-wharf and to Uncle Nicolo's dingy little gondola. But before she had time to draw back, Ditta had seized the Princess and, without waiting for screams, had gagged her with the twisted handkerchief about her head. Lifting her as though she were a basket of oysters instead of a Princess of the realm, Ditta half-pulled, half-carried her the next few feet, and there Uncle Nicolo was waiting. He took the squirming bundle—an easy matter for one who caught cuttle-fish—and the next moment his gondola had disappeared, while Ditta—with the Princess' ring on her finger—was back at the pavilion.

It had all occurred so quickly that no one was aware of anything happening; no one noticed the substitution. But Ditta was breathing hard with anxiety as well as with her exertions, and she was relieved when she heard a whisper, " There she is ! "

" Where ? " The second voice was cruder and less cautious.

" There," replied the first, and Ditta recognised the cool, suave tone. " You can't miss her. The one in rags, with the blonde hair." (Ditta was glad she had remembered to whip off her kerchief-cap.)

" Ah—! The one with the seal-ring on her right hand ! "

" Right. And don't let her out of your sight for a moment ! "

The fireworks began again. Serpents of fire wriggled across

the lagoon; umbrellas of light shed a whistling red and gold rain. The world turned blue . . . emerald . . . violet. . . .

Just before the second intermission, there was an outcry from the other side of the Piazza. " Someone's been stabbed ! " " An Englishman ! " " Stop them ! " " Help ! "

The confusion was well managed, thought Ditta; all is going as they planned. And now—

At that moment four hands grasped her, swung her off her feet, thrust a gag into her mouth.

" Not a sound out of you, my fine lady," said a rough voice, while a smoother one added, " If you come quietly, no harm will follow, but if you make a disturbance, it will be your last cry ! "

They did not know, as they lifted her into the patrician's gondola, what the smothered sounds might mean. They could not guess she was choking with laughter.

There was no light except a dark lantern in the gondola. But it was enough for Ditta. Even in the shadows she recognised the crafty Venetian noble, and the waves against the vessel told her they were headed beyond the channels. She would have to act quickly now. Luckily, she was not only a daughter of the lion, but a child of the sea.

Ditta, still gagged and bound, lay in a corner, writhing as though in pain. One of the men, a kindly faced ruffian, loosened the knots about her wrists and started to speak to her.

THE DONKEY OF GOD

"Don't trouble yourself," mocked the leader. "She's English, and the English cannot understand any language but their own—if they can understand that! But it scarcely matters. You can talk freely in any case: for even if she understood, she would never repeat it. We'll take good care of that."

Then, in a queerly accented English he said to Ditta, "You like ride in Venetian boat—yes?"

For answer, Ditta leaped from her corner, throwing all her weight against the opposite side. The boat lurched and the Venetian noble sprang backward to steady the pitching craft and himself. Ditta, who had worked her hands free, leaped again, this time at his throat.

"You little wild-cat!" he spluttered. "Take your claws off! I'll teach you! Here, Mario—!"

But Ditta slipped out of his clutch, dodged Mario, and was out on the rail in one fish-like movement. In her right hand was the small purse-bag she had torn from the Venetian's neck and this she held tightly. Then, as the two men caught at her heels, she dived.

The gondola headed about, taking after her. But she was in her element now. Besides, the black night aided her, speeding her on. When a burst of rockets brightened the water, she dived under the prow of the gondola, holding her breath until the dark intervals while the boat tried to locate her invisible body. She had never felt safer. She was a silver porpoise chased by a blind and bewildered whale. Sometimes, when the men pointed out a floating log and cried, " There she is ! " Ditta would be resting so close alongside that they could have touched her; sometimes she would actually put her hand on the stern of the gondola and let it pull her landwards. Finally, when she could see the lights of the Piazza, she struck off sideways, swimming partly under water, on a long angle towards the Doge's Palace.

The Doge was dumbfounded; the Grand Council blinked.
" Your tale is incredible, and yet I almost believe it," declared the Doge. " It is a serious crime you are alleging—high treason against the State—and I recognise the accused person from your description. An amazing story ! But have you any proofs ? "
" I thought you might want them," said Ditta. " So I collected as many as I could. You will find the English Princess with my Aunt Emmi and Uncle Nicolo over the market in the Rialto. You won't recognise the Princess at first, for she's in rags and most likely in tears, but her people will. Besides here is her ring."
The Grand Council nodded gravely, but the Doge permitted a smile to play about his heavy eyes.
" So war with England is averted," he said softly. Then to Ditta, " But we haven't identified the traitor yet ; though you,

THE DONKEY OF GOD

Signori," he added, turning to the Council, "must have guessed he was one of the Falieri."

"I have this," said Ditta, holding out a piece of linen. "It is the handkerchief they used to gag me and it is marked with an F. Besides, I thought it best to take this also." And Ditta offered the bag she had snatched on the gondola.

"But this is a miracle!" exclaimed the Doge, after he had examined the contents which seemed to consist of a single piece of parchment. "This is conclusive evidence—the document that reveals everything! How did you know it would be there?"

"Where else could it be?" answered Ditta, looking more than ever like the Princess and less like the fisherman's niece. "I heard him say this would be his death-warrant if it were found, and I didn't think he'd leave so dangerous a thing at home where some one might discover it by accident. He would never want it out of his sight. And so—" Ditta's gesture finished the sentence.

"Wait here a little moment, my child," said the Doge, and, at that instant he looked as kingly and as kindly as her favourite lion. The great curtains closed.

When the Council had re-assembled in the Great Hall under Tintoretto's immense "Paradise," the Doge made a speech, the like of which had never been addressed to any woman in the history of Venice.

DAUGHTER OF THE LION

"And so," he ended, "you have saved the State from bloodshed and terror. The Republic owes you much, possibly its very life; and it will not be ungrateful. Your family will be richly provided for; the house in which you live will have a tablet of honour; you and yours will come and go like nobles, without restrictions of any kind. As for yourself, you will receive a chest of silks and an annual reward of one hundred gold pieces. Is there anything else you may desire?"

"Please, your Highness, if I may ask it—"

"Yes, child," encouraged the Doge. "But what is your request?"

"A canopy for the lion in front of the Arsenal and a roof for the lion of St. Mark's. You see, they get so little rest—and there are too many pigeons nowadays."

So for years the people remembered Ditta. Every Ascension Day a huge hamper of golden pippins and damson plums and rich Dundee cake came from England to Aunt Emmi and Uncle Nicolo, while the Princess sent Ditta a box of rare finery and jewelled knick-knacks. Later Ditta visited England where she found a husband, and, for a wedding-present, they were given the estate of Rosslyn. But no one forgot Ditta and her lions.

THE DONKEY OF GOD

Until the fall of the Venetian Republic, a silk canopy was kept above the seated lion in front of the Arsenal. And to this day the lion of St. Mark's has a roof—and a royal one—of his own.

ROME

ROME

ROME

ROME, so the favourite proverb goes, was not built in a day. Nor, the saying should add, was it finished in twenty centuries. " The Eternal City," with its continual re-shaping, will not cease being built until eternity. Starting as a forum for the citizens of one small tribe, Rome has become an Empire, the seat of a vast religion, a world-centre where every race may be seen and every tongue may be heard. The noise of its fountains—and there are almost as many fountains in Rome as there are soda-fountains in New York—is like the babble of endless debate in a thousand dialects. If the sound does not echo the eternal argument of its inhabitants, it may be the immortal laughter of its departed but not wholly defeated gods.

One must " see " Rome leisurely. Nothing can be gained by rushing about, getting a glimpse of this and a glance at that, until it all seems like a jig-saw puzzle with some of the pieces missing. There are, of course, people who see everything on schedule and whose eyes are the eyes of a clicking motion-picture camera. There is the story of the young lady who boasted that her family " did " Rome, past and present, in a day. " A day ? " asked her friend, incredulously. " But how was it possible to cover the art, the history and the associations in a few hours ? " " Well, you see," answered the rapid traveller, " we divided it up. Mother did the galleries; father went over the ruins; and I took in the general atmosphere."

Rome is not one city at all, but many civilisations. Sometimes these different Romes—ancient Rome, mediaeval Rome, modern Rome—are found side by side; sometimes they are built one upon the other. For example, some of the greatest historical ruins are wedged between the ghetto of the Middle Ages and a bargain business section of to-day. Some of the classical buildings have been made over into churches; the church of S. Costanza existed originally as the tomb of Constantine's daughter and S. Maria sopra Minerva was built (as the name indicates) above and around the temple to Minerva.

Your first look at Rome is likely to discourage you. There is so much to see and so little time to see it; it is all so scattered and half-concealed, so sublime and so ridiculous. You feel the confusion rather than the glory, like the artist Yoshio Markino who wrote, " I am rather disappointed with Rome. It was a little raining yesterday. The effect was awfully bad. I prefer Newcastle-on-Tyne far better. . . . Rome is just like an old lion's den, where its own dwellers passed away a long

ROME

time ago, and now you cannot see even a single bone of lions, only small mice are playing in it."

But, in two or three days, the glories shine out of their backgrounds and the lions come back to their dens. You soon learn where to find the exact colour of Rome which pleases you best. It may be the antique world that centres about the Forum and the Colosseum; the romantic parks and the greater gardens of the Villa D'Este at Tivoli; the tritons and water-horses that never cease spouting and splashing in a hundred fountains; the countless public and private museums, from the endless Vatican to the compact Borghese, that historic pleasure-house; the splendour of its court festivities, or the richer colour of its street-life. You will find whatever you have heard, read, or dreamed of here.

Animal stories were popular two thousand years before Brer Rabbit and his younger brother, Peter, became household heroes. One of the happiest of these is connected with the founding of Rome and never suffers in re-telling.

Among the descendants of Aeneas, that heroic wanderer, was Rhea Silvia, a vestal virgin. The god Mars loved her and was the father of her sons, the twins Romulus and Remus. But Rhea Silvia's uncle was a jealous king. Fearing to lose power through his heirs, he had Rhea buried alive and, throw-

THE DONKEY OF GOD

ing the twins in a wicker basket, set them adrift on the Tiber.

" Let them swim, if they can," cried the king. " If they drown, it will not be my fault. The rising river will be to blame ! "

But the river rose higher than ever—so high and fast that, before the basket could sink, it was washed ashore. There, on the banks of the Tiber, the infants lay, crying with hunger, sick with cold.

At that moment, a she-wolf passed by. Having lost two of her cubs, she took pity on the babes. " They're so naked," she murmured to herself. " So hairless, so helpless. And so homeless. I'll take them home to the other children."

So she did. Romulus and Remus were brought up as part of the she-wolf's family. They drank milk from her breast, played with the young wolves in the cave, grew stronger and more cunning than any of the cubs. One day a pack of hunters came through the forest and, with many dogs and daggers, made short work of the she-wolf and her young. But Romulus and Remus, faster than the others, slipped through the circle, and escaped.

For a while, they lived with a herdsman who tried to bring them up as his own sons. But they were too wild for such a life. They wanted to rend and run ; the smell of sheep made them snarl and think of blood. One day, when they were in their most wolfish mood, a friend of their mother's came by.

ROME

Something about their features woke his wonder and, questioning the herdsman, he guessed who they were. Without a moment's delay, he told the twins—now full-grown youths—of their royal origin.

" Blood ! " cried Romulus to Remus. " It's blood we must have ! "

" Yes," answered Remus. " Now we know what we need. King's blood ! "

The rest of the legend is short and dramatic. The twins found their native country, took up arms, and avenged their mother by driving her murderous uncle from the throne. The people offered the kingship to the two heroes, but they were still restless. Remus wandered to the north and his son Senus founded the city of Siena. Romulus, however, returned to the place of his rescue. There, in the groves among the seven hills, he established the city that was named in his honour : Rome. And, after his death, he was worshipped as a war-god whose place was among the immortals.

The founding of Rome, according to this legend, occurred in 753 B.C. The next thousand years is a red record of wars, invasions, sacks, burnings and rebuildings. The Gauls destroyed the town and were, in turn, defeated. The Etruscans

THE DONKEY OF GOD

defied the growing importance of Rome, and lost their independence. Year by year her power increased; one by one she subdued Spain, Egypt, Macedonia, Carthage. Caesar came, saw, and conquered all of Gaul. In the year 31 B.C. Rome became an empire and, for five hundred years after, ruled the Western world.

One can see little of that first grandeur now; most of it must be imagined. But what little can be seen compels something close to awe. Here, from the top of the Palatine, where Romulus erected the first cluster of houses, you can see the antique glory that crept up the seven proud hills.

The ancient world can be felt in a score of places, probably keenest in the Colosseum. Here, covering more than six acres, is the colossal amphitheatre where gladiators fought each other to the death, where strange animals, torch-driven through subterranean passages, were slaughtered and early Christians were sacrificed. Here sat Nero and the Vestal Virgins and sixty thousand other holiday-makers, roaring their approval when a lion was gored by a wild bull, or turning down derisive thumbs when a poor captive with a broken sword begged for mercy. And here, too, the moonlight comes through the great arches, framing the walls in silver, softening the stone, until the brutality is forgotten and nothing remains but beauty.

Since the fall of the Roman Empire, the Colosseum has

ROME

been used in a curious variety of ways. It was a fortress in the Middle Ages; an arena for bull-fights in the Thirteenth Century; a sort of quarry during the Fifteenth to the Seventeenth Centuries, furnishing building material for churches and palaces; a hospital during the World War; a factory where saltpetre was made; and, finally, a memorial to the martyrs who perished during the persecutions. It is worth noting that the Colosseum, as a building, was never finished; and yet, after nearly two thousand years, it still stands for the world's wonder.

Nothing can give a more vivid picture of the struggles of the early Christians than the Catacombs. Here is the reverse of the Colosseum and the great Roman Empire—here is the " other side " of the ruined splendour from which a new faith emerged. Instead of towering walls and arches of triumph, here are the underground passages where the persecuted believers had to hide and pray; here are the tunnelled tombs where they were buried.

Here, frescoed along dim corridors of earth are the oldest symbols of Christianity—the lamb, the dove, the fish—and here are the rough stone seats on which the first Popes were throned. You emerge from these crypts as if—transported to the days of the disciples—you might have come out of the grave with the ghost of Peter.

But none of the Roman ruins draws the visitor closer to

THE DONKEY OF GOD

antiquity than the Forum. It lies in a hollow between two hills (the Palatine and the Capitoline) and its marbles barely suggest that this was once the civic and religious centre of the Empire. Buried beneath the weight of centuries, used for a time as a cow-pasture, time has recovered its own again and the marbles tell the tales of many gods and changing grandeurs. The massive arch of Severus, the upstart ruler from Africa, faces the basilica of humble Francesca, Rome's favourite saint. The burial-place of Romulus marks the spot where he made peace with the King of the Sabines after the Romans had kidnapped the Sabine women. The temple to Caesar was erected on the site of his funeral altar, and in the very centre a group of laurel-trees throw their leafy tribute over the fallen columns. The arch of Titus recalls his conquest of Jerusalem, one of the reliefs showing his soldiers bearing the biblical Ark of the Covenant and the holy seven-branched candlestick. The three columns of the temple of Castor and Pollux—that most beautiful silhouette—revive the story of the well-known heroes who, after death, lived half the days under the earth and half among the gods, and whose attachment for each other can be seen in the skies where the two friends were immortalised among the stars as Gemini.

Some distance off stands another typical Roman relic, the Pantheon. You will visit this, not because it is the finest example of Corinthian style—which it happens to be—but because it is the only ancient building in Rome which has come through the ages perfectly preserved. Twenty-seven years before the birth of Jesus, it was founded by the Emperor Agrippa —you can still see his name cut in the stone of the portico— and it was dedicated to a group of mythical major gods. Now, as a church under the name of Santa Maria Rotunda, it has become the public mausoleum of kings by birth and kings by achievement. Here the mortal remains of Victor Emmanuel II and Humbert I lie in the same room with those of Raphael, a mere painter and son of a commoner.

But it is the Pantheon itself which is more impressive than its historic associations. The sixteen granite columns which make the portico, rear their weather-coloured stones to a height of forty-six feet, each column a single block of granite. The bronze doors are imperial at every inch. The circular interior is lit by a single opening, a Cyclop's eye in the centre of a dome which is finer than St. Peter's. The veined floor, the filtered light, the upward-reaching curve make us forget the petty problems of everyday; the ridiculous is lost in the sublime.

The Vatican is not merely a palace and the home of the Pope; it is a seemingly endless series of connected buildings.

THE DONKEY OF GOD

These buildings, erected at various times with little relation to each other, include gardens, chapels, twenty courts, about three hundred staircases. Its museums are the largest and richest in Europe; its rooms, halls and suites number more than one thousand—a complete city within a city.

The room that draws most visitors is the Sistine Chapel—so-called because it was built for Pope Sixtus IV—a chapel as large as a church. Here Michelangelo laboured for twelve years to perfect a design which is one of man's greatest glories. He complained continually and toiled with superhuman energy. He was a sculptor; painting, he said, was not his business. One of his enemies, expecting that Michelangelo would disgrace himself by failing to carry out the plan, had persuaded Pope Julius to give the sculptor the commission. Yet when a number of assistants came to help him finish the massive undertaking, Michelangelo sent them away and completed the huge creation alone—the one work which was to be completed as he had conceived it. The ceiling alone took four years. Lying on his back on the high scaffoldings, his eyes were strained from insufficient light, his face and clothing spattered with paint, his limbs so cramped that he never regained full vigour; taunted by his enemies, unrewarded by the Pope, harassed by lack of funds, the titanic genius rose above physical and mental distress. Agony is, doubtless, reflected in Michelangelo's masterpiece, but it is the agony of a god. Here,

ROME

as in the tale of Jacob or in the music of Beethoven, man wrestles with the angel. Living meanly, the Prometheus of paint achieved magnificence.

The Sistine Chapel is Michelangelo's Bible. It is vast and sombre; its prophets are profound and powerful; its figures grow ever larger in scale and conception; the mind is noble, intense and inexhaustible. Contrast this work with the work of his fellow-painter in the adjacent *Logge*, a work known as Raphael's Bible, and the difference in the two men is revealed at once. Raphael's bright designs are the reflection of a happy nature; they are not grand, but they are gay. Even the larger and more dramatic subjects in the five halls known as the *Stanze* radiate with Raphael's spirit—a spirit that tasted more joy in a month than Michelangelo knew in a lifetime. If all other records were destroyed, Raphael's would be enough to re-create the entire Renaissance.

Nor should the fame of these two make us neglect the other rooms and chapels. There is the gem-like chapel of Nicolo V decorated by the Blessed Angelico. There are the wall-paintings of Botticelli and Perugino—most of them, alas, in the Sistine Chapel where visitors, intent on Michelangelo, never notice them. There are the apartments of Alexander VI, embellished by Pinturrichio, where the frescoes come alive with tame monkeys, and mischievous kittens, and mild gazelles staring reproachfully at the Elders, and mythical birds and

THE DONKEY OF GOD

beasts springing up like curious flowers in the flowering grass.

But paintings and painters are only a small part of the Vatican. There are the vast galleries; the halls packed with priceless gifts from the potentates of all the earth; the library of books and manuscripts by the hundred thousand in illuminated cupboards; the rotundas, each of which contains some world-famous statue; the array of sculptures where no guide is needed to point out the famous Laocoön group, the Discus-Thrower, the early Apollo Belvedere and the much later Perseus, hewn when Canova tried to restore the Greek purity in the Eighteenth Century.

But here you begin to weary—and not without cause.

It is impossible to get more than a faint idea of a few of the marvels of mediaeval Rome—unless you want to spend the rest of your life going from one church to another. On my part, I shall list only the more important ones and merely mention why they are noted.

There is, first and foremost, St. Peter's. It is futile to describe, or attempt to describe, its setting and its stateliness. It stands, a crown-jewel above a royal colonnade, tremendous, timeless, enshrining the grave of Peter, the humble fisherman. Now, as Peter, the bronze effigy is a throned monarch; millions crowd to kiss the worn toe. The plain " rock " on which a church was built is more gorgeous in purple and gold than any palace.

ROME

St. John in Lateran is known as the " mother and head of all churches " since it was founded by Constantine in the Fourth Century. Here, according to tradition, the first Roman Emperor to become a Christian was baptised; and, in the building opposite, are the *Scala Santa* (" the holy stairs ") said to have come from the house of Pilate. This flight of twenty-eight stones, continues the legend, was ascended by the Saviour, and sinners who follow in his steps—ascending the stairs only on their knees—are granted indulgence from penances.

S. Maria Maggiore is the oldest church in Rome dedicated to the Madonna; its mosaics are the finest examples of early Christian art; its proportions are breath-taking, and it contains fragments said to be from the manger in which Jesus was cradled.

S. Paoli Fuori le Mura (" St. Paul's Outside the Walls "), an enormous edifice more like a temple than a church, was erected over the tomb of St. Paul. The old altar is surrounded by a modern canopy upheld by four gigantic columns of alabaster, and along the aisles are mosaic-portraits of all the Popes, beginning with St. Peter—all except the one which legend has hinted was a woman : Pope Joan.

S. Clemente is a preservation of a primitive basilica; it is built on top of two earlier structures, one of which used to be a temple to Mithras, the sun-god of the Persians. S. Maria del Sole, a round bird-house of a church, was once a temple to Vesta. S. Croce in Gerusalemme is said to have been founded by St. Helena; it is so-called because it contains a portion of the True Cross—but more of this in the tale that follows.

S. Maria sopra Minerva was richly erected, as said before, on the site of a temple to Minerva. It contains Michelangelo's youthful " Christ with the Cross " and it was in this church that Galileo, aged seventy, was tried for heresy for saying that the earth moved about the sun, was forced to recant, and rose to his feet saying, " And still it moves ! " S. Pietro in Vincoli has, as the name declares, the chains in which St. Peter was held a prisoner; but it is sought chiefly because it contains Michelangelo's titanic Moses, whose great force and majestic figure make the church look small. S. Maria in Aracoeli is noteworthy for its long flight of stairs, its rich marbles, and the *Santissimo Bambino*, or " the Holy Babe."

Hundreds of years ago—even legend does not say how many—there came to Rome a peculiarly shaped piece of wood. Legend refuses to say how it got there, but it was a piece of olive-wood. Some said it was from the Mount of Olives; others went further and declared it was a cutting from the very tree against which Christ rested in Gethsemane the night before the Crucifixion. Then some one noticed that it had the shape of a small child, and a wood-carver used his knife until every one could see the features of a smiling babe. Henceforth it began to work miracles, restore the lame, banish fevers, cure the afflicted.

To-day it is the most honoured relic in Rome. The effigy is continually in demand. It is carried in a private coach by the monks who guard it; people prostrate themselves when it passes; it is said that the fees which the monks collect for its practice are greater than any physician's in Rome. When not in use, the image is locked in a safe over the altar of a darkened chapel, enclosed in a glass case, swathed in silks, literally buried in jewels and votive offerings. On the head of the Holy Babe is a gold crown studded with pearls. It needs only one thing—a Hans Christian Andersen to tell the fairy-tale of the wonder-working, gem-strewn figure that started life as a piece of olive-wood.

There is another world in Rome, scarcely a less lovely one. It is a world of spacious squares, poetic parks, romantic rambles of gaiety and sadness combined, where many and memorable ghosts inhabit the side-streets. In modern Rome, backed by the Aurelian wall, is the Protestant cemetery sacred to all poetry-loving hearts because it holds the graves of Shelley and Keats. The tombstone of the latter is so modest that it

THE DONKEY OF GOD

does not even bear his name—only "A Young English Poet," and underneath, as he had requested of his friend Severn, "Here lies one whose name was writ in water." Inconspicuous though it is, that little tombstone dwarfs the pompous pyramid of Cestius which looms above the wall.

But modern Rome is not all memories, by any means. The Pincio, that most friendly of parks, makes citizens of every nationality feel immediately at home. Situated on a hill overlooking most of the city, crowned by the gardens of the Villa Medici, it is Rome's chief pleasure-ground. Here the scarves of the native nursemaids, gay with "Roman stripes," are brighter than the perennial borders; there, on the terrace of the Casino Valadier, the mixture of international elegance reminds one that Rome is as much a world-centre as ever. No gardens have ever been better designed to frame a sunset. Ilex and the poet's laurel grow in classic groves; drooping acacias open their green tents; the Pincian hill—especially n late afternoon—blossoms into a beautiful unreality.

You descend into a slightly less romantic world, but not a less vivid one: a world of fantastic streets where a scornful Fiat motor-car may be held up by a contemptuous team of oxen; of proud villas and shabby tenements where the poorest house is always painted the gaudiest; of old walls which are pasted over with posters calling your attention to the latest candidate or the last word in soups; of an Amusement Park,

ROME

with " all-the-fun-of-the-fair " rubbing shoulders with Trajan's Forum.

Or there is the world of the restaurants which run from one extreme to the other. For example, you may dine at the Ulpia, which is very charmingly placed in an old Roman tomb, where the kitchens are situated in the crypts and (to keep the antique atmosphere) the bill-of-fare is inscribed on long rolls of funeral parchment. Or you may feast fully as well, and far more economically, at Alfredo's—if you can find the side-street to which most of the world has wandered. Alfredo is not only a master-chef, he is a magician, a maestro of hospitality, an impresario. Five minutes after you have entered, he will put before you the choicest of his viands and the treasures of his heart—the latter being his autograph-books in which the Great Ones of our day have placed their signatures, credentials and caricatures with expressions of their delight in Alfredo's *fettuccini*. No matter what else you order, you must not neglect the *fettuccini*—not unless you want to ruin Alfredo's happiness and cheat yourself out of a real experience in food as Art.

" But," you say, as the *fettuccini* is brought to the side-table where Alfredo is waiting, " but it's only noodles ! " Ah, my dear friend, it may look like noodles, but no one on this side of Elysium has ever served noodles like these, noodles so rich and melting, so light and unearthly, so wreathed in

THE DONKEY OF GOD

glory—no one except Alfredo. Watch him as he anoints the airy ribbons of *paste* with double butter; observe how he fluffs and finger-curls and marcels the plateful with the gold fork and spoon which he proudly admits were presented to him by Douglas Fairbanks and Mary Pickford; sharpen your wits and your appetite as he adds the final touch in the form of fine-grated parmesan and puts it before you with his benediction. Then offer up your prayers of thanks. . . . It has always been a puzzle to me how the gods on Olympus could ever have enjoyed ambrosia before the days of Alfredo.

Or there are the famous side-walk markets which spring up and disappear like brilliant mushrooms. To see these, you must be an unusually early riser. But you need not lose sleep to see the most famous of them, the Campo de' Fiori; you need only be in Rome on a Wednesday. Every mid-week, a dozen squares are combined for the sale of everything under the sun—and several things which must have grown under the mysterious light of the moon. Here is a perfect forest of fruit, flowers and—strange though the combination seems—fish. Fowl, too; great pendants of chicken and necklaces of singing-birds—beccaficos, those fig-pecking nightingales—which the Italian would rather eat than hear. Flowers overflow into the alleys where the Rag Market is at its giddy height. Here you can buy—*can* buy? you are actually compelled to buy—such " rags " as altar-cloths, priests' robes, old damasks, hand-wrought leathers, medallions with holy relics, watches carried around the huckster's neck like braided onions, laces, lingerie, linens, genuine and false antiques jumbled together, fine jewels and the poorest plated ware from Pforzheim—books, bracelets, broccoli, barrettes, beauty lotions—all sold in a commotion that would make a circus seem a silent affair.

But, whether in the noisiest section or in the quietest corner, Rome will capture you. No matter how long or short your stay, you will sigh upon leaving. You will scorn the superstition about the penny and the traveller who wishes to return, but you will follow it. On the eve of your departure, you will drop a coin in the fountain of Trevi as a tribute to Neptune, the god of ocean voyages. Then, say the believers, you will get your wish, and some day, somehow, you will return to Rome. Destiny—or Neptune—will bring you back.

THE HOLY CROSS

UG

A VIVID BLUE LIGHT FELL UPON HIS FACE

THE HOLY CROSS

VANNI was the curse of the countryside. He was a robber and an outlaw. In this he seemed to resemble Robin Hood, but actually he was his opposite. Where Robin Hood was generous and open-hearted, Vanni was greedy and hard as granite; where the rogue of the English greenwood robbed only the wealthy, the Italian bandit stole from the poor as well as the rich. Vanni would snatch a basket of eggs from a peasant as readily as he would waylay a merchant for his mare and his money. But the chief difference was in this: Robin Hood was a devout and God-fearing worshipper; Vanni feared no one and believed in nothing.

He and his band might appear suddenly in any of the central provinces, but their chief headquarters were in the hills and caves of Tivoli, just outside of Rome. Not even the bravest of citizens dared pursue him to his stronghold. The tales told by the unfortunates who had happened on Vanni's lair and had, somehow, survived were enough to keep armies away. So great was Vanni's power and so brutal his use of it that

THE DONKEY OF GOD

no one ever referred to him by name. Far and wide he was known only as " the Terror of Tivoli."

As he grew older, he grew more grasping. It was rumoured that he was the richest person in the kingdom and that his treasures were greater than the Pope's. There seemed to be nothing left for him to possess. And then, one day, he had a strange desire.

" To-morrow night," he told his second-in-command, " we go to Rome. I have the wish to own the fragment of the Holy Cross by which these priests set such store."

The lieutenants shuddered, yet they did not dare betray themselves for fear of their godless leader.

" I know it is a foolish whim," continued the Terror. " It is nothing but a bit of wood—no different from any other piece, in all probability. Yet I am disposed to have it. If it works miracles for me, I shall keep it about; if it does not live up to its reputation, I shall use it to kindle a fire. To-morrow night, then. And we shall see what we shall see."

Now the story of the Holy Cross was very much as follows :

When Adam and Eve were driven out of Paradise, the Lord wept. He pitied their weakness and saw the miseries their children would have to endure. At the last moment, He almost relented. But God's word is Law, so the Angel at the gate sent Adam and Eve out into the world, allowing them to take nothing out of Paradise except one thing : a branch of the tree

THE HOLY CROSS

which had been the cause of their downfall. This Adam planted and soon the branch grew into a tree and bore fruit. It never reached the size or glory of the original Tree of Knowledge, but it had magic properties, and Adam's children became wise—as God intended. In the time of the Flood, Noah cut it down, and with the timber he built the Ark which saved mankind. For three thousand years the wood was exposed to wind and weather, sun and rain; but it never rotted. From this wood, Moses made his wonder-working staff and Solomon constructed the Temple. When the Queen of Sheba came to Palestine, she touched one of the pillars and prophesied that the wood would bring death to the King of kings and that the kingdom of the Jews was coming to an end. Thinking the prophecy referred to him, Solomon became alarmed and buried the wood in a deep marsh.

There it lay until the days of Jesus. When the time for his crucifixion came, the wood was found floating on the Pool of Bethesda. It was taken out, cut, and carried by Jesus. And on the cross made from the Tree of Knowledge, death came to the King of kings.

After the Crucifixion, the cross was lost for another three hundred years, until the Empress Helena, mother of Constantine, had a vision which led her to unearth all three crosses. But how to tell the cross on which the Saviour had hung from the crosses of the two thieves? The Empress had a dying

THE DONKEY OF GOD

woman brought to the place where the three crosses were standing. Nothing happened when the woman touched the first two, but as soon as she embraced the third, she was instantly healed and restored to full strength. The identity of the Holy Cross being proved, the Empress caused it to be encased in silver and placed in the most sacred of shrines.

From that time on, the Holy Cross passed from hand to hand. Kings fought for it; heathen monarchs captured it; it was despoiled, hacked, broken into bits. Finally nothing was left but a few pieces, and these pieces were distributed among the greatest churches of the world. Set in crystal, enclosed in caskets of gold, they were venerated as the most sacred objects in Christendom.

One of these holy relics was in the church of Santa Croce in Rome—the very church Vanni was planning to rob.

"We will leave here shortly after sundown," said the Terror of Tivoli. "The night promises to be chill and dark, and we will arrive at Rome in plenty of time. By daybreak we should be back here with the treasure in my hands."

Leaving instructions to be roused at sunset, the Terror lay down for an hour. It was crisp sunlight of the following day when he woke. The hour was noon.

"What is the meaning of this!" he roared. "Some one is going to be tortured for last night's folly! Come! Confess! Who is to blame?"

THE HOLY CROSS

But no one knew. Shortly before the going down of the sun, a great tiredness had fallen on the camp. Within ten minutes, every one had sunk into a heavy slumber—a sleep from which the men had just been wakened by the sound of the Terror's voice.

" Here ! " he shouted. " Let me have that wine ! "

But he could detect nothing unusual in the taste. Nor had the food been tampered with. No one ventured an explanation.

" It looks like devils' work," muttered the Terror. " But man or devil, it doesn't matter; it shall not happen again. Make your preparations. We leave at once—and let the devils try us in daylight ! "

They were at the gates of Rome before nightfall. Within an hour they had dispatched two of the guards, tied up six others, and disposed of the rest in the usual manner. By midnight they were in front of Santa Croce.

But a surprise awaited them. As they approached it, the church shot into flames. So fierce was the fire that the skies turned white; so intense was the blaze that the bandits' beards were singed though the air was frosty and though they stood a square away. They dared not venture closer. The flames did not come from any one part of the building, but burst out from every window with the force of an explosion. All night long the fire raged, and all night the Terror cursed and kept his distance.

THE DONKEY OF GOD

Yet in the morning, when the first bell was rung for Mass, the flames died down as suddenly as they had shot up. The air cleared; there was not the slightest smell of smoke. And the church of Santa Croce stood firm and fair, without a smudge to mar its marbles.

"Devils' work again!" swore the Terror. "Some one will pay for tricking me! If I find out—!"

His men were whispering among themselves. But the Terror cut them short.

"No more of this!" he threatened. "To-night I'll have that cursed trinket in spite of fire or flood. My heart is set on it now, worthless though it is. I'll get that relic if I have to demolish the church and strike down the Pope himself!"

That night it was calm and sweet-smelling. The fountains of Rome sang like the nightingales, and the nightingales rippled their liquid music like the fountains of Rome. There was no other sound.

Before ten o'clock the Terror and twelve of his picked men were in the church. Nothing had happened to oppose him; no one, not even the sacristan, was to be seen.

"Queer," he muttered. "I expected trouble. Perhaps the devils are discouraged. They know, once I've made up my mind, I can't be thwarted."

His men were stationed at every door to guard against a surprise attack. Three of them even descended into the crypt

THE HOLY CROSS

with torches to search for hidden foes among the tombs. But it was unnecessary. Not a hand was raised against the Terror as he ascended the high altar. Nothing disturbed him as he prised apart the iron grilles except a vivid blue light that fell upon his face. For a second the Terror was startled; then he saw it was caused by moonlight shining through the robe of Jesus. " Just a trick of stained glass," he muttered to himself, and shrugged his shoulders.

By now he had broken through the double casket which held the sacred relic. In another moment, the crystal container was in his hands; within it, he could see the piece of precious wood from the most Holy Cross. In spite of himself he trembled slightly, and his fingers shook as he stuffed the priceless thing into his wallet.

But when, at daylight, he opened the leather wallet, it was empty. There was nothing whatever in his bag—no fragment of the cross, no crystal container, not even the silk cloth in which it had been wrapped.

" Devils again ! " swore the Terror. " No human hands could have performed this robbery. The bag has not been out of my grasp all night—and no one has dared come near me. But I'll have that devilish object if I die for it. More than ever, it must be mine ! "

Turning a corner at that moment, he was aware of a large crowd gathered about a ragged pilgrim. Without waiting to be addressed, the pilgrim lifted his head, looked the Terror straight in the eye, and spoke :

" When you have done three good deeds you will have your heart's desire."

" Who asked you for prophecies, you psalm-singing worm ! " growled the Terror. " Prophesy a full meal for yourself, why don't you, you wretched scarecrow ! Besides," he ended grimly, " good deeds will never get me the thing I've set my heart on—only bad ones." And, roughly elbowing his way through the people, he hurried on.

He had not gone a hundred paces when he caught sight of a disturbance. There was much scrambling, shrieking and milling about. The centre of the commotion seemed to be a dog.

" Mad dog ! " the shout went up. " Mad dog ! Stone the beast ! Tear him apart ! Kill him ! "

Whatever else the Terror may have been, he was no coward. The dog was in front of him, muscles twitching, jaw slavering. Vanni felt for his dagger, drew it half out of its sheath. Then he spat in disgust.

" Idiots ! " he said. " Can't you see that the dog isn't mad at all ? He's been hurt. He's howling and trembling with pain."

And, bending over the animal, he examined it with expert fingers. The dog suffered him to open the quivering jaws without protest.

" Ah ! That was it ! " cried the Terror. " A sliver lodged in

THE HOLY CROSS

the back of his mouth. Here is what made frightened fools of the lot of you!"

And, extracting the splinter, he threw it away and went on. Just as he turned the next corner, he noticed another group of people thicker than the first. But, instead of screaming, the people here were wailing softly.

"It seems to be a day for crowds!" murmured the Terror, as curiosity pulled him to discover what had happened. What he saw was a group of women clustered about a well.

"It's her child," sobbed one of the women, pointing to another. "The little one fell in a while ago and there's no way to get her out. Besides," she shuddered, "they say there are Things down there."

"They say! They say!" mocked the Terror. "What won't they say! And what won't you simpletons believe! Are there no ladders here?"

"None long enough to reach even half-way," said the woman.

"No ropes?" he inquired.

"Nothing but this one—and who would trust himself with that? It's far too short. And what there is of it is old and frayed."

"Here," called the Terror in his sharpest tone of command. "Give me that piece. If fools would only talk less and act more—! But then they wouldn't be fools!"

THE DONKEY OF GOD

It did not take him long to snap out his few instructions. He tied the treacherous-looking piece of rope around his waist and, fastening the other to a tree that grew next to the well, let himself over the curb. For a few feet he managed to secure a kind of support on the rough stones, but soon there was no foothold and his whole weight hung on the rope. Yet the cordage did not split; not a strand broke. More than that, the rope lengthened—or seemed to lengthen—until the Terror touched the very bottom of the well. There he found the whimpering child, grasped her firmly and gave the signal. As soon as he was on the surface, the women rushed toward him, but he waved them off.

" One more fool's child who will grow up into one more fool to clutter the earth ! " he jeered. And, as if to make up for time wasted, he hurried by them. The twilight was chill ; flakes of snow sharpened the winter air.

" What manner of crowd will I find next ? " he asked himself, half humorously, half scornfully. " All things come in threes, and it wouldn't surprise me if next I should be intercepted by a whole congregation of devils. Well, let them come, with Satan at their head. I'll turn the tables and do the tormenting. I'll plague them ! I'll torture them till they tell me how to get the relic, for get it I will ! Let them come ! "

But he saw no more crowds. Nothing stopped him as he hastened to the secret meeting-place at the edge of the woods

THE HOLY CROSS

on the road to Tivoli. Nevertheless, he stopped in some surprise as he drew near the appointed spot, for not one of his twelve lieutenants was there as planned. Instead, there was an old man huddled upon the ground.

For a moment, the Terror thought a corpse lay at his feet and—though he would have denied doing it—he crossed himself. Then, as he saw a thin smoke of air leave the old man's lips and shape itself on the chill dusk, he knew the beggar was not quite dead.

" Well, it's no business of mine," he muttered to himself. " If fools will lie down on a cold night and freeze to death it's their own fault—especially if they are old fools ! "

Yet he did not move. The Terror shifted from one foot to the other.

" I might as well wait here as anywhere else," he muttered. " And as long as I'm waiting, I might as well make a fire for myself. And as long as I'm having a fire, I might as well build it close to this old bag of bones and let him share it."

The Terror gathered an armful of fallen branches, piling them tent-like on each other.

" Let us have a real blaze while we are about it," he said, and tore down a great bough from a dead tree.

But before he could start the flames, the fire lit itself. The glow was not gradual, but seemed to blaze from every branch at once. And, as the Terror started back, the dying man stood

THE DONKEY OF GOD

up. In the light of the fire, the Terror could see he was not an old man, but a young and gentle one. It was the pilgrim who had prophesied to him that very morning.

"Come here, Vanni," said the pilgrim, and the Terror did not know whether he was more moved because of the sweetness of the voice that called him or because it called him by his name. "Come and see what I have for you."

The pilgrim held out both hands. There was an object in each of them.

"See," the beggar went on, "this is the splinter you removed from the dog's throat. It is a curious splinter, Vanni, for it was once a thorn in the crown which pierced the brow of Jesus. And this, Vanni, is a frayed bit of rope. A brave deed was done with it to-day. But no human hands except yours have held it since its cords bound the wrists of the Saviour. And this piece of wood with which you warmed a frozen beggar—" here the pilgrim smiled, stretched out his hand and took the broken bough from the flames—" it is a brand plucked out of the fire. And you, Vanni, are the branch that is saved from burning. Look—take it—for it is yours."

For a moment no word was spoken, no breath rose. Nothing could be heard but the sound of a man falling upon his knees.

"Oh, Vanni," went on the pilgrim. "You are a poor sort of Terror. You thought you believed in nothing: you thought all

THE HOLY CROSS

men were fools. But you fooled yourself. Your mind mocked at goodness; your mouth scorned kindness; yet your heart leaped at the chance to be noble. Three times to-day you could have moved toward evil, but—without hope of return—three times you chose to do good. Therefore, here it is. Here is the Holy Cross!"

The tale breaks off here. Some say that the Terror disappeared that night and his band fled to distant countries. But in Tivoli a few recorders insist that he lived to a rich and revered old age. They will tell you that he fed the hungry, erected homes for the homeless, turned all his property over to the poor. He enlarged the church of Santa Croce and placed the sacred relic in a finer shrine than it ever had. Instead of Vanni the Terror, he became known as Giovanni the Restorer.

As he lay dying he had, they say, a dream.

"It is the same vision I had that night when I sank to my knees," he said. "As I looked in the eyes of that pilgrim, I looked into His heart. And there I saw high heaven unfold, while a voice sang, 'What you have done to the least of them you have done to Me.' It was Paradise I saw—and I shall see it soon again. There, perfect once more, without lacking a leaf, stands the Tree from which the Cross was made. It is greater than ever, for every good deed is a new branch upon it. Under it sit the Saviour and the saints and the prophets, and the fruit drops into the hands of all men. And the roots of the Tree are in every heart."

THE END

Made in the USA
Coppell, TX
24 March 2025